Linda is ten years old as she positions herself in the seat in front of Momma's dresser and plays dress up. She and I have done this many times before, but today Linda is alone as she talks to herself while putting on Momma's makeup and clip on earrings.

As she looks in the mirror to brush her hair, she can see the double bed a few feet behind her and the walk-in closet to her left. All of a sudden Linda sees the bed shaking and moving, but she doesn't see anyone in the bed! She is afraid and wants to run, but she doesn't turn around, out of fear that whatever is there will grab her.

Linda continues looking in the mirror and brushing her hair as she pretends nothing is wrong and tries to think of a way to get out of the room. Whatever shook the bed is between her and the door, which heightens her anxiety.

Suddenly Linda sees the closet door near her slowly open, and she doesn't see anyone standing in front of it! Now she is even more frightened and wonders if it is a ghost. Linda's heart beats wildly, but she continues talking to herself as if she is still playing dress up and waits for an opportunity to flee.

Linda watches through the mirror as the closet door slowly closes by itself. The instant the door is shut, she jumps up and runs out of the room...

Swamped by Ghosts

J. Katherine Till

Bookends Publications
Norfork, AR

Swamped by Ghosts
Copyright © 2014 J. Katherine Till
All Rights Reserved

Bookends Publications
Norfork, AR

No part of this book may be reproduced or transmitted by any means, electronic or mechanical, including photocopying, recording, or by any information storage and retrieval system, without written permission from the author, except for the inclusion of brief quotations in a review.

The views and opinions expressed within this book are that of the author, and do not necessarily reflect that of the individuals mentioned in this book, unless otherwise specified.

ISBN: 978-1500833787

Illustrations and back cover photo of J. Katherine Till
by Steven Till, Sr.

All nature photos, including the cover photo, copyright Joseph Adair.

Photo of the LeBeau mansion/Friscoville Hotel (p. 151) now in public domain, taken by George François Mugnier (1857-1938). Originally found at
http://www.thepastwhispers.com/Old_New_Orleans.html

Photo of the LeBeau mansion (p. 159) copyright Corey Balazowich, used with permission and gratitude.
https://www.flickr.com/photos/coreyann/2217577708/

Photos of individuals from family archives.

Editing, Layout, and Design
Alathea Daniels
(870) 656-9082
windsong@mtnhome.com

Acknowledgments

Special thanks to God and the Holy Spirit for guiding me as I wrote this book, and for giving me the courage to speak out about a subject most people go out of their way to avoid.

Much appreciation goes to my sister Linda for helping me edit *Swamped by Ghosts*. She also supplied details of our childhood experiences and family history. The book includes ghost encounters Linda and her husband Carroll have had in their home for the past forty years.

Many thanks also go to other family members who shared their ghostly phenomena, thus enhancing the book even more.

Sincere gratitude to my editor, Alathea Daniels, for the many hours she worked editing and designing *Swamped by Ghosts*. I am also grateful for the friendship that has formed through our work together.

I greatly appreciate my husband, Steve, for his much needed support, ideas, research, and for assisting me in numerous other ways while writing the book.

Without everyone's help, the publication of this book would not have been possible.

Contents

Introduction xi

1. **Life as We Knew It**. 1
2. **Embracing the South**. 9
3. **An Unusual Beginning** 13
4. **Ghost Encounters** 51
   A Spirit Follows Us 59
   We Barely Escape 61
5. **Knock, Knock, Who's There?** 66
   A Living Doll. 81
   Batteries Not Included 85
6. **Spooked on St. Michelle Avenue** 89
   Mirror Manifestation 93
   A Night to Forget. 97
   Strange Sounds in My Room. 99
7. **Family Lore** 107
   The Amityville House. 110
   Double Occupancy 110
   The Spirit of Masion Madame 115
   Beyond the Grave. 117
   Skeletons in the Basement 119

8	**Gouauxst Avenue** 121
	Now They See Him—Now They Don't 127
	A Terrifying Spirit 128
	Back From the Dead 130
	Daddy & Betty's Ghost 137
	Screams in the Night 140
	A Cloud of Lights 142
	Something Light for Supper 143
	Four Men and a Baby Ghost 145
9	**A Ghost Town** 146
	The LeBeau Mansion 150
	Ghosts in the LeBeau Mansion 153
	Sleepless Nights 156
	Another Mansion Nearby 160
	A Spirit Attacks Me 160
10	**No Safe Place** 164
	A Spirit in Our Car 172
	Our Kids Are in Danger 174
11	**Haunted House of the Rising Sun** 176
	A Woman Ghost 192
	Second Floor Exile 194
	The Boy Ghost 198
	A Welcomed Visitor 201
	A Haunted Ship 206

	The Mansion Inspired a Song	211
	Shannon Almost in a Movie	212
	Shannon an Extra Cast Member	212
12	**Can't Get Away From Spirits**	214
13	**Spiritual Activity**	229
	Signs to Indicate the End of the Age	231
	Ways to Defeat the Devil	235
	The Ten Commandments	240
	Things the Bible Will Do	241
	Prayer	242

About the Author 243

Ghost Books by J. Katherine Till 245

Joseph and Angela Adair 247

Introduction

Everything in this book actually happened and is portrayed according to the recollection of those involved. Many unusual things have occurred in my family, and some of them are of a paranormal origin. All of them took place in the marshy lands of southern Louisiana, thus giving the title of the book, *Swamped by Ghosts,* two meanings.

I did not intend to write this book. I initially wrote some ghost stories to put in a genealogy book that I was writing about my family, but then I realized that there were enough ghost stories to create a separate book—which eventually became the first printing of my book, *Haunted House of the Rising Sun.* This book was composed of stories about a beautiful mansion in the New Orleans area that I lived in with my first husband and our two children. What started out as a dream come true became more like a nightmare, as we witnessed hauntings almost every day of the four years we lived there.

People who enjoyed reading *Haunted House of the Rising Sun* asked if I had other ghost stories. Without knowing this, my brother Joseph Adair and then my cousin Nora Jewell both suggested that I write a book about our childhood experiences. This inspired me to write the book you are now reading, *Swamped by Ghosts*. Ghost encounters of other family members have also been included in this book.

Some of the stories in both of these books are funny, a few seem unbelievable, and several are downright frightening—but all of them are true. So sit back and try to relax as you share this journey with me through incredible accounts of the supernatural.

Chapter 1

Life As We Knew It

Using the surname *Adair*, I traced my family lineage back to the early days of Great Britain and discovered that the motto on our family coat of arms is "Loyal au Mort," which translates to "Loyal Unto Death."

The motto originates from a fair battle between one of our ancestors and another knight. Our ancestor beheaded his opponent and won the victory.

This causes me to wonder if the death that brought about this seemingly innocent motto, and other things family members may have done over the years, have anything to do with some of the spirit encounters our family has had. But mostly, it seems to be unsettled resident ghosts we happen to encounter in some of the homes we move into.

We come from a good lineage, but even the best of families have things about their past that are better left buried and forgotten, better known as skeletons in the closet. Our family is no exception.

Our great grandfather on our paternal side was George Washington Adair. He was of Irish blood, and a descendant of the Cherokee Indians as well. His son was Everett Lee Adair. When Everett's son (who would one day be our father) was born into the family, he was given the same name.

Daddy was born in September of 1923. He was the son of a casket maker and a homemaker, and he was the eldest of two children. He and his sister grew up with their parents in Texarkana, Texas, and they enjoyed a middle-class lifestyle. Sometime in Daddy's youth he acquired the nickname E. L.

Everett Lee Adair, Jr.
Our father in his youth.

Daddy was very close to his mother. However, she died when he was just sixteen years old, and her death had a devastating effect on him. Daddy became depressed. He began participating in illegal activities and was eventually arrested.

Daddy did not get along well with his father to begin with, so when Daddy was arrested, Granddad came down hard on him. This pushed them even further apart.

As soon as Daddy was of legal age, he joined the Navy to escape his father's demands of perfectionism, but also because he wanted his father to be proud of him. Unfortunately, Daddy was only in the Navy for a short period of time. He was dishonorably discharged after becoming romantically involved with an officer's daughter.

When Daddy returned home, his behavior spiraled in a downward slide. He began frequenting bars and billiard halls, which led to his drinking heavily and dating lots of women. Daddy was soon known as a "ladies' man"—a regular "Don Juan."

Momma was born in March 1926. She was the daughter of a farmer and homemaker, and a descendant of the Cherokee and Choctaw Indians.

She was the fifth born of eight children, and she grew up in the rural town of Red Water, Texas. Momma and all of her siblings had to work in the cotton fields with their father so they could make enough money to barely get by. Momma's father made one dollar per day, and each of the children were paid fifty cents per day.

During the Great Depression, there were many days that all the family had to eat was homemade biscuits. Momma and her siblings only went to school a few months each year, because they had to work in the cotton fields. Momma began looking for a way out of that life.

Ollie Viola Jewell
Our mother as a young woman.

When Momma was fifteen years old she met Daddy, who was nineteen years old, and they began dating. After a whirlwind courtship, they married in 1943 at ages seventeen and twenty, respectively, and they quickly began having children.

Their first child was born after nine months of marriage. She had beautiful red hair and Daddy's blue eyes. She quickly became the center of Daddy's world.

Seventeen months after their first child was born, Momma was expecting another baby. Momma gave birth to their first son, and Daddy insisted they name the baby Jonnie Lee.

A few months later, Momma discovered that Daddy had been living a double life. Not only did he have a wife and two children—he also had a very active social life with numerous other women, and he used the name "Jonnie Lee" in his alternate life.

Momma was devastated to learn that her son was named after Daddy's alternate persona and that Daddy had never stopped dating other women.

Momma wanted to leave Daddy, but she was expecting another baby and didn't know how she could support herself and three children. Twenty-two months after Jonnie was born, Momma gave birth to another precious girl.

We aren't sure when it started, but at some point Momma began seeing other men and drinking alcohol.

Our three older siblings had difficult childhoods due to our parents' behaviors, but out of respect for my siblings, I will not discuss elements of their lives unless they pertain to an important detail of this book's story.

Eight years after their third child was born, Momma and Daddy moved their family to Shreveport, Louisiana, and began having their second set of children.

Linda was born in December 1956. She had stunning blond hair and blue eyes. Perilous things happened throughout our childhood, and there were times when God intervened on our behalf. When Linda was a baby, something happened that warranted such an intervention.

Momma was distraught with worry while driving with her four sleeping children in the car. They were homeless and in the middle of nowhere in northern Louisiana.

It was the end of the road for Momma. She had no money, and she didn't know where Daddy was. The radio blasted out a familiar song. All of the windows were open for lack of an air conditioning system. What happened next is astonishing. Sometimes when you don't know what to do, God steps in to help in a way you don't expect.

Giving in to utter despair, Momma glanced out the driver's window and saw a little angel sitting on the side mirror outside of the car! Then she was instantly transported to heaven! One moment Momma was driving the car, and the next instant she was standing before God's throne. Meanwhile, her physical body was slumped over the steering wheel while the car was still in motion.

God asked Momma if she was ready to go to heaven. He gave her a moment to decide. She didn't have to say a word, because God knew her thoughts. Momma wanted to return to her four children.

God said, *"It's not her time. She has to go back,"* and sent Momma back to earth.

Suddenly Momma became aware that she was back in her body and was slumped over the steering wheel of the moving car. Soon she realized they were thirty miles further down the road than previously. This means she was probably in heaven for about half an hour. Miraculously, the car didn't crash into anything. The angel must have been driving it so the children would be safe while Momma was taken to heaven. All four of them remained asleep and were unaware of the whole event.

Momma often spoke about this major event as we were growing up. After it happened, she was very glad to be back with her children. Then she bore two more.

I was born in February 1959, with chestnut hair and brown eyes. It was around this time that Momma began seeing a man that became a life-long love affair. He was from Houma, Louisiana.

When I was a year old, Momma convinced Daddy to move to Houma, and it was there that Momma gave birth to their last child. Joseph (Joe) was born in February 1961. He also had light brown hair and brown eyes.

Our oldest sister got married five months after Joe was born, and our second to oldest sister married in December of that same year.

About two months after our oldest sister married, she came to visit us in Houma and was disappointed but not surprised to discover that we were not there. We had moved back to Shreveport. It was not uncommon for Momma to move at a moment's notice without notifying family members or friends. She frequently moved to the same areas in order to be with people she was familiar with.

We lived in Shreveport for only two months. In November 1961, Daddy and Momma separated. Jonnie was fourteen years old and Linda was almost five. I was almost three, and our baby brother Joe was nine months old at that time.

Momma took the four of us to Long Beach, California, to stay with Uncle James (Momma's brother) and his family in a house they owned there.

My family always lived what my sister Linda describes as a nomadic, chaotic lifestyle. When we were growing up, we moved so often it seemed like we lived in almost every neighborhood in Houma.

Growing up in an alcoholic home caused our lives to be even more unstable, but two constants were ever present. First of all, we knew our mother loved us. As a matter of fact, as adults we discovered that we each believed we were Momma's favorite. To this day we still marvel over this, because as parents we know that this could not have been an easy task. The second constant was that no matter what hell we were living, Linda, Joe, and I always had one another.

We struggled financially, though Daddy made enough money for us to be considered a middle class family. A large portion of the money went to supply our parents' heavy smoking and drinking habits. Ours was the life of a typical dysfunctional alcoholic family.

Despite all of the things we went through while living in Houma, I am glad our parents decided to settle there. I like the area and the people.

Chapter 2
Embracing the South

Houma is in southern Louisiana, and part of Terrebonne Parish. In other places these divisions are called counties. The city of Houma was founded in 1834.

The name Houma is derived from the Houmas Indian Tribe. The first inhabitants of Terrebonne Parish were Native Americans, but not the Houmas Indians. The first inhabitants were unknown tribes dating back hundreds and possibly thousands of years. Several Native American burial mounds were built by them around the parish, but over the years nature and man have destroyed the mounds. Human bones, pottery, and other items have been found in the dirt mounds of this dead culture.

When I was young, my family and I would sometimes visit one such mound, and we had fun sliding down the tall hill. Sometimes my brother Joe and I built a makeshift grass hut to play in at the top of it.

Our mother brought us to the mound because it was the only hill in this flat terrain to play on, and it got us out of the house for a while. As a kid, I didn't realize the significance of this sacred hill. Later I understood that the mound was more than just a hill to play on, and I wondered if we had disturbed the spirits of the Native Americans who were buried there.

These Native American settlers were gone by the time the European explorers arrived at the end of the seventeenth century. The next group of Native Americans did not arrive in Louisiana until the late 1700s.

In the 1600s, the Acadians, who would later become known as "Cajuns," began their journey from the rural areas of the Vendee region of western France. They settled in an area known as "Acadie" (now Nova Scotia, Canada), and after much hardship (which one historian has described as being similar to a modern day "ethnic cleansing"), some of these French settlers came to Louisiana in 1764. Soon hundreds followed them. Most of the Acadians who came in 1785 settled along Bayou Lafourche.

Right after the turn of the century, Louisiana became the property of the United States. Then new settlers came. Among them were the English, Irish, Italians, and others. Some of their customs were embraced by the Acadians.

At the beginning of the 1800s, almost every Acadian still spoke French, now known as Cajun French. French is still fluently spoken in many of the surrounding areas today.

Plantations line the banks of the bayous on the outskirts of Houma, Louisiana. The City of New Orleans was the main trade distribution hub of industry in southern Louisiana, and plantations were usually built along the waterways of rivers and bayous to the south and west of New Orleans to make the transport of goods easier.

When the slave trade was taking place in New Orleans, people from the surrounding areas came to the city to buy slaves to be used for their domestic and manual labor. The prospect of the seafood industry hadn't caught on yet. The parishes that surround New Orleans were mostly swamp land. They used the manual labor of slaves to fill in the land and to cultivate it so crops could be planted.

Around the 1980s, the world began to embrace the Cajun culture, mostly because of the delicious Cajun cuisine and the festive attitude of the carefree southern lifestyle.

Houma and the surrounding areas are steeped in Cajun tradition and culture. The area is known for its fabulous food. And who could turn down a good cup of coffee and donuts? The Cajun French call it "café au laite and beignets" (pronounced *café ah lay* and *ben yays*).

Like New Orleans, Houma is known for its Mardi Gras festivities and seasonal food festivals.

Houma is also known for its distinctive music, lively dances, fishing, and for the many swamps in the area. People there are known for their hospitality. They welcome strangers and sometimes offer them a meal. They will say things like, "Come sit for a while. Want something to eat? Want some coffee?" They enjoy a good conversation.

Although Houma is changing and growing, many of the people still make their living as their ancestors did. Among them are fishermen, crabbers, shrimpers, and trappers in this bayou country. Over the years many of them began working in the oil industry and became ship builders.

Chapter 3

An Unusual Beginning

A log shaped like an alligator.

When we are young, our father, Lee, drives an 18-wheeler and later becomes a tugboat captain. His job takes him away from home for weeks at a time. Sometimes while off duty he can be found at the local bar. His constant companion at home is his beer, and he is drunk most of the time.

We try to stay away from him as much as possible. When Daddy is drinking, he becomes verbally aggressive toward all of us, but he also becomes physically hostile toward Momma.

It terrifies us when Daddy hits Momma. We become very protective toward her. On numerous occasions Linda calls the police. When the law enforcement officers arrive at our home, they talk things over with Daddy. He promises not to do it again, so the police don't arrest Daddy and the cycle repeats.

As an adult, Linda admits that as a child she would pray every night for Daddy to die because she couldn't stand all the arguing and fighting.

Throughout our childhood, Daddy moves in and out of our lives each time he and Momma separate and get back together. One day he's there, and then suddenly he is gone, and we might not see him again for a year or two.

Our mother, Ollie, has worked her whole life and juggles work, home, family, friends, and a boyfriend into her hectic schedule. Momma does most of her drinking at home.

When Daddy does live with us, and he is at work, Momma often goes out dancing and partying with her longtime boyfriend. Sometimes Momma plays cards at home with her friends. Alcohol flows freely at our home while bills go unpaid, and uprooting our family to yet another residence is common.

Two months after we move to Long Beach to Uncle James's home, we move back to Houma and we rent a small house for a while. Two double beds are in the living room for us to sleep on, and a dresser sits against the opposite wall. Our older sister is glad when she finally locates us.

Daddy and Momma get back together and buy a brick house on Holiday Drive in Houma. Momma is happy because it looks like we have finally settled down.

Momma likes their bedroom more than any room in the house. If someone would walk into that room they would know what her favorite color is. Everything in there is red except the floor! There are red curtains, a red bed spread, a red lamp, red walls, and even a red telephone.

Sadly, she doesn't get to enjoy her new room long. Momma is heart broken when we lose our home because Daddy can't pay the house note.

Mom & Dad in 1962.

It is 1962. Linda is five years old, I am three, and Joe is one when we move from our brick home and into a rental on West Main Street in the township of Bayou Cane. It is on the outskirts of Houma. The bayou is behind our house.

Animals frequent our yard and enjoy the benefits of the water. Occasionally a slow-moving snowy egret is seen at the water's edge.

Most of the time there are alligators lounging in our back yard while we play outside. They don't bother us, and we don't go near them—not knowingly, anyway.

Alligators lie out in the sun, and they remain very still for extended periods of time. Often they are there for hours, and sometimes for days. They blend in with the territory and look like cypress logs.

When alligators are in the water, sometimes all you see is their nose and part of their eyes. Their eyes are closed most of the time, which conceals them even more. The eyes of the alligator reflect the light at night, causing them to glow red.

An Unusual Beginning

Alligators can grow to ten feet or more, and they are very strong. Joe is so small that an alligator could eat him whole. We don't realize the danger we are in as we have fun playing in our back yard.

Linda likes to play alone most of the time. Almost every day for the past few months, she has been sitting straddled on a log at the edge of the water as she plays with her plastic tea set.

Today Linda is having a great time, talking to herself as she carefully places the tea set on the log in front of her, pretending to serve tea to her imaginary friends.

Linda notices her tea set move a little when Momma suddenly comes running out of the house screaming, "Oh my God! Linda, get away from there! That alligator is going to eat you!"

Linda has no idea what Momma is talking about. She looks around and doesn't see an alligator.

Then without warning, Linda and her tea set begin to slowly sink into the water, and she realizes that it is not a log that she and her tea set are sitting on. It is a huge alligator!

Momma is shaken up pretty bad as she grabs Linda from the back of the alligator and runs into the house.

We move from the house not long after this frightening incident has occurred.

It is a wonder that the alligator didn't attack Linda on all of the days she sat on the back of it. Maybe the alligator had just finished eating and was not hungry when it relaxed at the edge of the water, or perhaps Linda's guardian angel was working overtime trying to protect her.

In 1963, Jonnie turns eighteen years old and joins the Navy. He comes home to visit once in a while, and his visits are always memorable.

An Unusual Beginning

It is 1965. Linda is eight years old, I am six, and Joe is four when we move to Maxine Street. Soon Daddy and Momma separate again, and the three of us are taken to live with an adult cousin and her large family in Texas. We end up being there for seven months.

Our parents get back together, and we are excited when Daddy comes to get us.

It is good to be back in Houma. The surroundings look the same, but things in our personal lives have changed. We don't recognize Momma when we get home. She got her hair cut short while we were away, and it makes her look different. The Momma we knew had long hair. The house we are brought to is also different. Daddy and Momma moved while we were gone. Now they live on Garnet Street.

We are surrounded by strangeness, and we feel uncomfortable. The three of us feel awkward as we sit on the couch for hours at a time without moving.

Our behavior and coolness toward our mother must upset her, but she doesn't show it. Gradually we recognize Momma's mannerisms and realize that she is our mother.

We have lived in eleven different locations so far in our young lives, which includes four different states. There are a lot of changes, but we learn to adjust to them.

We are still living here when Jonnie comes home for one of his visits from the Navy.

I am puzzled the next morning when I open my eyes and see a kitchen chair sitting on top of me! The chair is in an upright position, with the legs resting on the bed on both sides of me. If someone were to sit in it, their feet would be in my face.

I call Momma to come get the chair off of me, and all of us have a good laugh during breakfast as Jonnie tells the hilarious story of how the chair got on the bed. He was sleepwalking during the night when he saw that I was uncovered. Jonnie thought he put a blanket on me, but it was a chair instead.

We have to move out of houses we live in over the years because Daddy doesn't pay the rent, but circumstances are different when we are forced to move from the house on Garnet Street.

Hurricane Betsy comes raging through Houma on September 9, 1965. After crossing Florida Bay and entering the Gulf of Mexico, she re-strengthens, growing into a Category 4 storm.

At the time Betsy hits Louisiana, the wind speeds are one hundred fifty-five miles per hour, which is about one mile per hour below Category 5 strength.

The huge storm continues northwestward, moving into Barataria Bay on that first evening. It makes its second landfall at Grand Isle, Louisiana, just west of the mouth of the Mississippi River, where it destroys almost every building.

The storm travels upriver, causing the Mississippi River at New Orleans to rise by ten feet. The Army Corps of Engineers Hurricane Protection Program comes into existence as a result of Hurricane Betsy.

The almost Category 5 hurricane hits the area where we live from 8:00 p.m. on September 9, 1965, to 4:00 a.m. the next day. For eight long hours our parents don't know if we will live or die in this massive storm. What makes it even more frightening is that Hurricane Betsy comes to Houma at night, with raging winds of up to one hundred thirty to one hundred forty miles per hour.

With Jonnie being home for a visit, he is forced to ride out the storm with us. Daddy is drunk and is arguing with Momma about where we should stay during the powerful storm. Daddy wants to bring all of us to the tugboat he works on. It is docked a few blocks away. Momma thinks we will be safer staying in the house. Then the storm arrives in full force.

The howling hurricane-force winds make eerie sounds as they tear at our roof. The strong winds and torrential rain cause a few ceiling tiles to fall onto Linda's and my double bed. It frightens me, because I had just climbed out of the bed after Momma had called out for me to come in there with them.

When I go to tell our parents what happened, I am told to get under the kitchen table with the rest of the family. Not long after this, there is an awful racket as our house is suddenly raised up from the cinder blocks it rests on.

All electrical wiring, plumbing, and the gas line are ripped from the house as it becomes airborne with us inside of it! I feel like Dorothy in the *Wizard of Oz* movie, only this is really happening.

A few minutes later, our house is put back down with a thump about three feet away from its original location. The house is now in the empty lot next door. None of us are injured, but it is a frightening experience for all of us.

Our parents realize that we need to get out of the house, because it is unsafe. When the wind dies down enough, all of us head to the front door.

Swamped by Ghosts

As we step outside, the wind is still so strong that Linda, Joe, and I are blowing sideways as the adults carry us to our light green, mid-1950s Chevrolet.

Our parents must be horrified that we have to go out into the powerful storm. Trees have fallen down everywhere, and Daddy is still drunk as he dodges live power lines that dance across the road. He is also arguing with Momma again, saying that we wouldn't be in this predicament if we would have gone to the boat like he wanted to.

It is a wonder that we even get to Momma's friend's home on Holiday Drive. While in their home, a large tree branch falls on the back glass of our car and shatters it.

We are forced to move from our house because of the damages incurred upon it. The garage apartment behind us was turned completely upside down during the storm.

Broken dreams.

Hurricane Betsy has brought about more than a billion dollars worth of damage, which causes her to be nicknamed "Billion Dollar Betsy." The huge storm has killed seventy-six people.

While Hurricane Betsy brings havoc to our town, our family is also torn apart. Daddy and Momma can't get along, and they break up again. Daddy blows in and out of our lives like numerous tropical storms. He blows in, creates chaos and destruction, then he blows out until the next storm arrives upon his return. We don't know where Daddy goes each time he leaves.

We are refugees, and we are forced to stay at the Levron Park in Houma for two weeks after Hurricane Betsy. Uncle James and his large family are also driven from their home and are staying at the park with us.

We have ice chests, but we are having a hard time trying to find food for all of us. Everyone is hungry when we drive to a small neighborhood convenient store one day and purchase candy bars. It is all that is left on the shelves to eat.

We rip the paper off of the candy as soon as we leave the store, but as we are about to shove it into our mouths we discover maggots throughout the candy! We remain hungry while maggots eat our only source of food.

Our lives have been turned upside down as we struggle to survive. But we are kids, and we learn to deal with the situation.

There is a lot of devastation at the park from the storm, and we have to wait a few long days for the ground to dry enough for us to play on the equipment. Excitement builds up in us kids when that day arrives. All of us look like horses jumping out of

Swamped by Ghosts

the starting gate at a race as we run in different directions to the variety of playground equipment.

A few other people have come to the park to let their children play. Joe and a little girl decide to get on the old-time metal merry-go-round. No one sees the downed, live electrical wire that is dangling from an overhead tree and onto the merry-go-round.

Both of the young children jump onto the merry-go-round—and the electricity immediately shocks them! Uncle James quickly kicks Joe off of the merry-go-round and saves him from electrocution, but no one is close enough to help the little girl. The mother is devastated as she holds her lifeless child.

Danger seems to lurk in every place we move. We aren't even safe at a children's playground.

Everyone is grieving over the loss of property, homes, and lives. Hurricane Betsy will be a haunting memory for years to come. Piece by piece we try to put our lives back together.

Linda is nine years old, I am seven, and Joe is five in 1966 when we move in with our older brother Jonnie and his wife Betty on Palm Avenue in Houma. It is by the bayou. Betty's parents live only half a block up the street from us.

Linda and I have a frightening experience one night while living in this house.

We decide to sleep in the narrow hallway. It is the coolest part of the house because a fan is in the attic opening. A door is on both ends of the hall. With both doors closed, the small area is like a closet.

We spread our blankets on the floor and sit on them while we play with our dolls. Then we lay face up on the blankets as we get ready to go to sleep. Linda and I glance up at the ceiling fan above, and to our horror we see the outline of a man through the blades of the attic fan! Our first thoughts are that a ghost is in the attic, and that it is going to get us.

We scream at the top of our lungs and panic as we try to open the hall door. Fear intensifies when we realize the blankets are blocking the door. Frantically we try to kick the blankets out of the way and pull on the door at the same time. It seems to take forever, but we finally manage to get the door open.

We never find out what or who was in the attic, but we are afraid to play in the hall after this frightening experience. I am glad when we move from this spooky house.

During Hurricane Betsy, many people fled into their attics to escape the strong storm, only to die there from the rising water. The bayou is right behind this house. I wonder if the ghost of a parishioner haunts the attic.

(Years later, this home became an oyster house. I am curious to know if other people experienced anything paranormal in the house, thus making it unlivable.)

We move to Main Street during the same year of the fan experience, 1966. Our lives seem to be settling down—for now, anyway.

I am captivated by the spirit of Mardi Gras as the parade passes right in front of our house, and we have fun as we string our own beads with broken ones we collect from our front yard and the edges of the street right after the parade ends.

Easter arrives soon after this, and we have an Easter egg hunt in the large yard. After dark, we have a great time creating our own Easter egg hunt in the house. There are lots of places to hide the candy and boiled eggs, especially in Momma's closet.

One day Momma gets angry when she slips her hand in the pocket of her coat and discovers a rotten egg nestled inside of it.

Dad and Mom, Linda, and Me, with Joe in the back.

I like this rental, though it is creepy living next door to a funeral parlor. It feels weird to know that there are dead people next door. Death is a neighbor, and sounds of sorrow are always on our doorstep.

Being curious kids, sometimes Joe and I stand by the fence that separates our yard from the driveway of the funeral home and watch as the hearse pulls up to the side entrance of the building. We continue looking as they carry the body of the deceased person into the building.

Other times we witness the frequent flow of families coming to make preparations to bury their loved ones. A wake soon follows.

As a child, I wonder why they call it a wake—if they are waiting for the deceased to wake up, or if they are there *in case* they wake up. I also question what happens to people after they die.

(Years later I wondered if spirits of some of the deceased lingered around the funeral home, and if they were in our house or yard while we lived there.)

Death is a constant reminder of our mortality and that life is fragile. Around this time there is a death in our family. Our paternal grandfather dies of a heart attack in his home town of Texarkana, Texas. It is my first experience with a person I know who has died, and I am deeply affected by it. Now I understand why the people Joe and I see at the funeral home are so sad.

Linda is ten years old, I am eight, and Joe is six in 1967 when we move into a garage apartment on Buron Street. It is in the middle of town. Our house sits on top of the garage.

This means another change for us and another school to attend, but we learn to adapt to our circumstances. Another thing that doesn't help our situation is that our parents separate again not long after this.

*The garage apartment on Buron Street.
Our bedroom is on the left.*

One day Momma and another adult bring us to eat ice cream at the Dairy Cool. Other kids are with us, which includes the girl who lives next door to us. She is between Linda's and my age. Linda also invites one of her female friends from school to join us.

We are having a great time—when the conversation takes a turn, and Momma concocts a plan. She issues a dare to us kids that we won't walk through the graveyard that night. The graveyard is at the end of our street.

It is ironic that we lived next door to a funeral home and played on an Indian mound, which is an Indian burial ground. Now we live down the street from a graveyard. Death seems to follow us.

The adults offer to buy us something as a reward if we make it to the other side of the graveyard. The offer is tempting, and the challenge sounds fun. We decide to take them up on the dare.

An Unusual Beginning

Night arrives, and Momma drives us to the graveyard. There is no changing our minds once we exit the car, because as soon as we get out, Momma drives away and goes to the other side of the graveyard to wait for us.

With only the moonlight to help guide our way, we set out across the spooky-looking gravesite. About halfway through the eerie graveyard, Linda's school mate trips on an old wrought iron cross and cuts her knee. Some of us stay behind to help her.

Linda's friend limps along as we continue the quest. Then something happens that frightens all of us half to death. Linda screams as she suddenly disappears into the ground! We scream and run because we think something got her.

I am torn in two directions as I try to decide whether to continue running to the safety of the car or go back and get Linda. My conscience overrides my fear, and I join the other girls as they turn around to go help her.

I am cautious as we enter the area where Linda has disappeared—knowing that I, too, may succumb to the perils of the graveyard.

We soon discover that Linda has fallen into an open grave. The depth of it is twice her height, with no ladder or steps to usher her out. Linda is trapped in the blackness of the hole. She becomes frantic and yells, "Get me out of here!" Linda is grossed out about being in a grave.

Lying on our bellies, we reach down into the darkness and feel for Linda's hands. We grasp her hands, then her arms, as she scurries out of the deep dark hole that has consumed her.

All of us successfully make it to the other side of the graveyard. We breathe a sigh of relief as we catch our breath. Then we quickly jump into the car.

The adults are laughing hysterically and making sport of our adventure. Soon laughter overtakes all of us as we discuss the triumph of our accomplishment. We vow never to do this again, no matter how tempting the dare.

When Momma hears of the things that happened to Linda and her friend in the grave yard, she realizes it wasn't such a good idea after all.

Later I wonder if we disturbed the spirits of the deceased when we ran by and over their graves. Some of the graves were below ground, but most of them were encased in an above-ground tomb because of the high water level in this southern state. Usually it is the wealthier families who can afford to have an above-ground tomb.

The towering tombs had formed a maze that concealed those who were ahead of us, and the above-ground graves were so close together that it was hard to maneuver around them or see where we were going in the darkness of night.

When we agreed to do this challenge, we hadn't realized there would be so many obstacles ahead of us. The graveyard looks a lot different when driving past it during the day.

Right before Linda took the following two photos in May 2012, a fence was built around the graveyard. I wonder if the fence was built to keep vandals out, or because others have attempted to walk through the graveyard at night. Unknowingly, we may have started a neighborhood tradition years ago.

An Unusual Beginning

The graveyard we ran through.

Another view of the graveyard.

Around the time of this frightening graveyard experience, we start noticing things in the house disappearing. Unusual things like blankets, cans of Vienna sausage, potted meat, and beer are among the missing items.

Momma blames us for taking them, but we have not done it. Being a child, I don't wonder who could have taken them. I just know that I didn't.

The house looks secure when we return home from being out, and none of us notice any signs of illegal entry. The situation is puzzling, but I don't think much about it.

One day Joe and I are playing outside while Momma bakes a cake. Momma and Linda ride to the store to buy some things while the cake cools. Joe and I don't go with them, because we want to continue playing with the kids in the yard behind our house.

When we go inside later, Momma fusses us because a piece of the cake is missing. She blames us for taking it, and isn't convinced when we tell her that we were outside the whole time. I would have loved some cake, and understand why Momma thinks we took it. We were the only ones at the house when it happened—or were we?

We begin finding answers to the mysterious things that are going on in our home, and Linda gets the shock of her life in the process when she and Joe decide to play hooky from school.

I love school and want to go even when I am sick. Linda and Joe don't like school, and they stay home every chance they get. Today is one of those days.

Momma tells Linda and Joe that if they stay home they must remain in separate rooms in the house all day. She wants them separated, so Linda is placed in Momma's bedroom while Joe stays in the room the three of us share.

Linda positions herself in the seat in front of Momma's dresser and plays dress up. She and I have done this many times before, but today Linda is alone as she talks to herself while putting on Momma's makeup and clip on earrings.

As she looks in the mirror to brush her hair, she can see the double bed a few feet behind her and the walk-in closet to her left. All of a sudden Linda sees the bed shaking and moving, but she doesn't see anyone in the bed! She is afraid and wants to run, but she doesn't turn around, out of fear that whatever is there will grab her.

Linda continues looking in the mirror and brushing her hair as she pretends nothing is wrong and tries to think of a way to get out of the room. Whatever shook the bed is between her and the door, which heightens her anxiety.

Suddenly Linda sees the closet door near her slowly open, and she doesn't see anyone standing in front of it! Now she is even more frightened and wonders if it is a ghost. Linda's heart beats wildly, but she continues talking to herself as if she is still playing dress up and waits for an opportunity to flee.

Linda watches through the mirror as the closet door slowly closes by itself. The instant the door is shut, she jumps up and runs out of the room.

She wants to tell Momma what happened, but she refrains from talking about it out of fear that people will think she is crazy. Linda also realizes the possibility that Momma won't believe her and will try to make her go back in there. She dreads going back in that room after what she saw in there.

Linda doesn't want to be alone, so she sneaks past Momma and goes into the room with Joe. She doesn't tell Joe about what happened in Momma's bedroom, and she hopes that her fear is well hidden. Linda doesn't want anyone to make fun of her. She has to deal with this frightening experience alone.

Soon Linda's fear becomes a reality when Momma finds her in our bedroom and tries to make her go back into her room. Linda refuses to go back in there and argues with Momma about it. She is adamant and determined not to go back into that room. She is pretty strong-willed and persistent, and Momma gives Linda her way.

When evening comes, Linda sits on Momma's bed and talks to her while Momma gets ready for a night out. Daddy is out on the tugboat, and Momma has plans for the evening that don't include us. A babysitter is coming here to watch us.

Momma puts on makeup and jewelry, and she heads to the walk-in closet to get her evening attire. Linda's heart races as Momma opens the closet door. She desperately wants to keep Momma from going in there. Linda is afraid Momma will have to confront what had gone into that closet just hours ago.

As Momma steps into the closet, Linda is terrified, and she thinks, *Oh my God! Oh my God!* Linda doesn't know what may be lurking in the closet. All she knows is that something went into that closet earlier today. She wonders if it is a ghost, since she didn't see a reflection of anyone in the mirror. She regrets not telling Momma about what happened in her room.

Linda lets out a sigh of relief when Momma casually walks back out of the closet with her clothes. She is glad nothing bad happened to Momma while she was in there.

This experience scares Linda and makes a lasting impression on her young mind. She is determined that she doesn't ever want to be in that room alone again.

Soon Linda's friend and her older sister come over to babysit us, and the frightening incident is pushed out of Linda's mind by the excitement of seeing them.

Momma leaves, and all of us get comfortable as we slip into oversized t-shirts that Dad had given us to sleep in. Then we sit at the kitchen table and play Monopoly. The noise level rises as we laugh and cut up.

When Momma returns hours later, she and Joe go to sleep in her bedroom while we continue playing the game.

At two a. m., I am tired and ready to go to bed. My place of sleep for the night is on the couch. All four of us had planned to sleep in our bedroom, but they may stay up playing Monopoly all night. It doesn't bother me because I am a sound sleeper, and I like being near the girls.

I need a blanket to cover up with, and ask Linda to go with me to get one out of Momma's closet. Linda and I have been afraid of that closet lately, and we have an eerie feeling that someone is watching us when we play in Momma's room. I am glad that Linda agrees to come with me, and that I don't have to face this fear alone.

Linda walks right behind me as we enter Momma's darkened room. Then I bravely head to the closet, because Linda is with me and Momma is asleep just a few feet from us—but mostly because I don't know that Linda saw something go into the closet earlier today.

Linda stands close by while I enter the walk-in closet to get the blanket. Seconds seem like hours as she waits for me to re-emerge.

Fears are played back in Linda's mind as she recalls the frightening experience she had just hours ago in this room. She lets out a sigh of relief as I come out of the closet unharmed.

As we walk back by Momma's bed, there is just enough light coming from the kitchen for me to notice that the bed covers are in a heap on the floor by Joe's side of the bed. I figure that he must have kicked them off the bed in his sleep.

I curl up on the sofa in the living room with the blanket and soon fall asleep.

The three girls are still playing Monopoly an hour later when Linda gets up to go to the bathroom. She enters the short hall and can see into Momma's bedroom through the open door. Unexpectedly, a movement in Momma's room catches Linda's eye. She glances that way and to her horror sees what appears to be a man by Momma's bed!

The man is on his knees, and the covers are all the way over his head. He is rocking back and forth next to Momma. Linda is puzzled, and wonders what is going on as she stands there watching this take place.

This confirms to Linda that someone was in Momma's room earlier today while she played dress up. She also realizes that she was only inches from harm. Now this intruder is in the bedroom with Momma and Joe.

Then without warning, the man reaches out and grabs Linda by her ankle! She starts screaming bloody murder and somehow manages to free herself from his firm grip.

Linda is hysterical now and continues screaming as she runs back into the kitchen where the other girls are. The two girls start screaming, though they don't know why Linda is screaming.

In a panic, all three girls try to get out of the front door at the same time, but they can't get the dead-bolt latch unlocked because of the commotion.

Linda is going nuts. She is so terrified that she stops trying to unlock the door and squeezes in behind the refrigerator to hide from the man. She thinks that if the man comes into the kitchen he may not see her back there.

Linda dreads what may happen next. It is so quiet in Momma's bedroom. Neither of them are making a sound or running out of the room. Something terrible must be going on in there, and the man may come after the rest of us.

The older girl finally gets the front door open. Then the three girls desperately run down the stairs screaming. They go to the landlord's house next door. Linda runs around his house and all the way to the front door. She starts banging and banging on the door, but nobody comes to answer it. In frustration and utter fear, Linda bangs on the door with all of her might. Superhuman strength, especially from a ten year old girl, tears the door from its hinges and sends it crashing to the floor with a thunderous boom.

The landlord and his family wake up alarmed when they hear banging on their door. He rushes into a defense mode as he scrambles to protect his family. They decide to call the police because they think Linda is someone breaking into their home.

When the police come, everything is explained to them by the three frantic, terrified girls. The police officers realize that an immediate response is warranted, and they climb the stairs of our house to rescue those of us still inside.

When the officers enter the apartment, they don't see the man, but they find Momma and Joe still unresponsive in the bedroom. The policemen rouse them and assist them down the stairs.

Through all of the commotion, no one realizes that I am still wrapped in my covers and sleeping on the couch in the living room! I am alone in the house with the intruder.

The police have the house surrounded, believing that the man is still in there. They are about to go back into the house to arrest the intruder, but they question Linda first about her encounter with the man.

As Linda tells them what happened, she notices what appears to be adults with wings on them across the street from our house. They are closely watching the activity going on.

Linda wonders why angels are here, and she also wonders if a play or some other performance is going on somewhere. This seems odd to her, though, because it is after three o'clock in the morning. It is too late at night for something like that.

With all of the commotion and many neighbors gathered on lawns and in the street, these adults with wings stand out from the crowd. No one but Linda seems to notice them.

(These were evidently real angels sent here by God to intervene in the situation. I feel secure in knowing that angels were here to protect us. Though everything was chaotic, it is comforting to know that God was in control. An angel may have assisted Linda with knocking the door down so the landlord would call for help. There is no telling what the angels may have done next if the policemen hadn't intervened. I thank God for guardian angels!)

Around this time it is discovered that I am missing, and they realize that I am still upstairs! Momma probably thought I was with the girls when they ran out of the house. The girls may have reasoned that I came down the stairs with Momma and Joe.

Someone goes upstairs to get me, and I am still half asleep when they put me down at the foot of the stairs. I am confused from being abruptly awakened, and I don't know what is going on. A lot of people are in our yard, and I assume there is a party going on. I am tired and don't want to be involved in it. I become angry that someone woke me up and begin stomping back up the stairs as I yell, "I'm going back to bed!"

Momma starts screaming. Others yell my name and say, "You can't go back up there!" The shouting and urgency in their voices cause me to fully awaken. I become aware of what is happening and quickly go back down the stairs.

I never thought something like this would happen to us. I shudder to think what probably would have happened to Momma and Joe if Linda had not seen the man in her room, or what he may have done to Linda if he hadn't lost his grip on her ankle.

The intruder could have attacked us tonight while Momma was not at home. He may have been waiting for just the right moment to bring havoc upon us, and tonight seemed to be the time to implement that plan.

It seems that his main goal was to remain in the house undetected, but he evidently had other sinister plans as well.

I wonder what may have happened to me if I would have entered the kitchen while the man was getting a piece of the cake

Momma had baked. I would have been in the house alone with the man.

The man had a chance to attack Linda when she was alone in the bedroom earlier today. He crawled across the floor so Linda wouldn't see him in the mirror.

He wanted to continue hiding in our home. The man had free reign of the house and could have caught any of us off guard. We had always felt safe and secure in our home—until now.

Neighbors are still gathered on the lawn as the police go into our house. They don't find the intruder in there, but they do notice that the stuffed Navy duffle bag belonging to our brother Jonnie was pulled into the hall and placed directly under the small attic entrance. They also notice several greasy fingerprints on the wall above the duffle bag and on the attic door. The officers realize that is probably where the man is hiding. The attic doesn't get searched because the police don't want to go up there.

What started out as a fun evening ends up being our worst nightmare. We don't want to go back into the house. We know that the man is probably still in the attic. We leave and go to the house of Linda's friend and her mother. It is the home of the two girls who came to babysit us.

The adults go back to our house the next day. Then they try to get us to go back, but we don't want to. No matter what the adults tell us, we don't feel secure in that house any more. We know that the man did not get caught yet, and the police didn't search the attic. He may still be in our house, or if he had left, he could have returned.

Linda can't go in, and she becomes so terrified that she starts screaming and crying. They don't make us go in, and they bring us back to Linda's friend's house. Then the adults go in our house and look around. They find a piece of cloth on the floor next to our mother's bed, and they call the police because it has a noxious smell on it.

They look under Momma's bed and see several empty Vienna sausage and potted meat cans, and a few empty beer cans all stacked up nice and neat underneath the bed. Now we know that there was a real, live boogie man under Momma's bed.

The police come and do a test on the cloth, and they discover that there is chloroform on it. It is a liquid used as an anesthetic—a medicine used to put one to sleep. It is obvious that the man planned to harm our mother, and possibly the rest of us, by bringing the chloroform into our home.

The man must have put the chloroform on Momma's face. He probably used it on Joe, too. That may be why they didn't respond to all of the screaming.

I probably didn't hear the girls screaming because I am a sound sleeper, or I may have ignored the screams because I thought they were still playing the game.

The attic is searched, and blankets are found spread out on the attic floor for a bed. Several empty cans of food and beer are scattered around it.

The police discover that the man who was in our house is a patient who had escaped from a local mental institution two weeks prior to this incident. They also become aware that the guy is guilty of murdering someone while he was in a psychotic rage. He is still on the loose and considered dangerous. This is probably why police officers didn't want to go into our attic when they entered the house to arrest the guy.

Just because someone is mentally unstable doesn't mean they aren't clever. This mentally challenged individual was keen enough to steal the chloroform, break into our home, and remain undetected for up to two weeks. This makes the situation even more disturbing, because this guy had been watching us come and go. He studied our house and our habits. We were in a serious situation and unaware of this man's sinister plans.

The trash he left behind indicates that he was there for quite some time. If he hadn't been so careless, we may have never known that he was there. A murderer was in our house, and we didn't even know it! He was hiding in the attic, under Momma's bed, in her closet, and no telling where else he could have been.

Who knows what drives a deranged mind to victimize innocent people. I wonder what voices were whispering in his ear, and what was driving him to do the things he did. The man may be haunted by things of his past or by memories of things he has done.

There is a spiritual war taking place all over the world—an ongoing battle of good versus evil and God verses Satan. We know what side this man was on.

Looking for a place to hide, the man seized the opportunity to enter our upstairs apartment by climbing onto Momma's car that was parked halfway in the garage and entering through our open bedroom window that was above the car. The man may have walked right past our beds while we were sleeping.

Momma parked the car in that spot because it was closer to the stairs and easier to pull in and out of the garage. She never thought someone would use the car to climb into our home.

We thought we were safe, and we always kept the windows in the house wide open so it wouldn't be so hot. The windows were all upstairs, and there was only a garage downstairs.

It was a convenient situation for the man. All he had to do was climb down from the attic to have access to our home. He could take anything he wanted. Whatever items he took would be blamed on us kids.

The only problem confronting him was that he had to be careful in selecting his opportunities. The aroma of Momma's freshly baked cake was probably too much for him to bear, and he had to go into the kitchen and get some of it. He probably thought all of us had gone to the store that day.

Momma wants to continue living in the upstairs apartment, and she tries for two weeks to get Linda to go back into the house. But Linda is so traumatized that she becomes hysterical every time she goes near the house. Linda is so upset that Momma ends up having to bring her to a psychiatrist. He tells Momma not to force her to go back into the house.

We never know what becomes of the murderer or if he is ever caught. We move from the garage apartment after living there only a few months.

Our parents' marriage falls apart and they separate again, which adds additional stress to our already hectic lives.

After staying with Linda's friend and her family for two weeks, Momma sends us to stay with our Uncle James and his large family, who have moved from Long Beach, California, to

St. Joe in northern Louisiana, to be near his wife's family. We stay there for two months.

Barnyard animals and vegetables from the large garden are the main source of food at Uncle James's home. Joe and I adjust to the primitive way they live, and we help catch bullfrogs from the large pond so our aunt can cook the legs. We enjoy eating the southern-fried frog legs. They taste like fried chicken.

It is a wonder that Linda doesn't starve, because she won't eat any of the barnyard animals that are killed. She feeds the animals, becomes emotionally attached to them, and doesn't want to see them butchered. For her sake, it is good that there is plenty of corn and snap beans in the garden.

The time comes to bring the pigs to the butcher. The day before they are shipped off, Linda finds out that they are going to be killed and becomes upset. She sneaks out of the house during the night, opens the gate of the pig pen, and sets the pigs free.

The next morning our uncle and aunt get angry when they find out that all of the pigs are missing. The adults and all seven of us kids get plenty of exercise running around trying to catch the pigs. There is a lot of squealing and laughing going on as the slippery animals evade capture. But to Linda's sad disappointment, all of the pigs are eventually caught and they still get sent to the butcher.

Five of us seven kids sleep in the same double bed. An outhouse is in the back yard for us to use, and a number three wash tub sits on the back porch for us to bathe in. Once per week the tub is brought into the kitchen. Our aunt heats pots of water on the stove and pours them into the tub. Everyone uses the same tub of water.

The girls go first, then the boys, then the adults. One by one, we strip and step into the wash tub. Our aunt leaves nothing to chance. She scrubs each of us until our skin glows bright pink.

Momma returns to get us after a few months in St. Joe, because school will be starting soon. Our aunt and uncle decide to move back to Houma with us. We load up Uncle James's pickup truck and our car, and we start the long trek back to southern Louisiana.

It is in the middle of the night when we get there. We have nowhere to sleep and very little money for a motel. The adults decide to look for an empty rental. They figure we can sleep in it for one night, and they'll contact the landlord the next day to make arrangements to rent the house.

We ride all over Houma, but we can't find an empty house. Then we go down the bayou to see if we can find one there. We finally find an empty house in Dulac, which is on the outskirts of Houma. The adults break into the house, and it seems perfect for us. We spend the night on pallets on the floor of the dark empty house.

The next day Momma contacts the landlord and rents the house. It sits back a ways from the highway and has a long porch that runs along the front and right side of it.

We live across the street from a bayou and an ice factory. The house is in a peaceful country setting. There are many moss-covered oak trees and cypress trees in this area, and sugar cane fields are seen along the highway.

Alligators and ever present mosquitoes are plentiful here. Some people in this area get used to the alligators, and feed them like they would a pet.

While standing at the edge of the water to feed the gators, female mosquitoes have their fill of warm human blood so they can fertilize their eggs. Thus, the cycle to breed more of the pests is completed.

"My favorite things are moon pies and tourists!"

All seven of us kids get to attend Vacation Bible School at a Baptist church several miles up the road. We have lots of fun, but Linda becomes stressed when it is time to leave. We are in separate classes because of our age differences, and we come from different exits when it is over. Linda frantically gathers all of us together, since she doesn't want us to miss our ride home.

The transportation is divided into two groups—those children who live up the road ride in one van, and those who reside down the road ride in another one. We are young and have not been told that we live "down the road," so there is some confusion until we figure that out.

We never miss a day of Vacation Bible School. I enjoy learning about God, our heavenly Father.

We are living here for about three months when Daddy shows up out of nowhere. We find out that he has been living in Washington State with our older sister. Our lives get more complicated when he moves in with us. Daddy is drunk most of the time. He and Momma argue constantly.

One night Daddy is extremely drunk. After a heated argument with Momma, he decides to leave. Momma tries to stop him, because she knows he is in no condition to drive. She is afraid he will either kill himself or someone else because he is so drunk.

Daddy won't listen to Momma. He pushes her aside and takes off in his truck. Momma is really worried, so she puts the three of us in her car and tries to catch up with Daddy to try and get him to come back home.

We go only about three miles down the road when we suddenly see a huge ball of fire on the left side of the road, next to the bayou. There is a fire truck and several police cars lined up along the highway.

Momma starts screaming and pulls onto the right side of the highway. She yells at us to stay in the car and takes off running across the street. A policeman grabs Momma and holds her back. The scene is like a nightmare.

A while later we see Daddy on a stretcher as he is being lifted into the back of the ambulance. We don't know if he is alive or not.

Momma jumps back in the car, and we follow the ambulance to the hospital. When we walk into the hospital we can hear Daddy yelling and cursing at people. We are thankful that he is alive, but embarrassed because of the way he is acting.

After a couple of hours, we find out that Daddy is fine. He has only sustained a few scratches in the accident. The police say that if Daddy had been wearing his seatbelt he probably would not have survived the accident. Because he wasn't wearing a seatbelt and his window was open, Daddy was thrown out of the truck. (Daddy could never be convinced to wear a seat belt after the accident. He would mention what the police had said and refuse to put it on.)

We go back home when Daddy is released from the emergency room. The next morning, Daddy announces that he is going back to Washington. He asks if we want to go with him.

Momma refuses to go, but Daddy convinces Linda, me, and Joe to go with him. We get excited when he tells us about the mountains and the schools, and we are eager to start a new life in Washington.

An Unusual Beginning

Momma begs us not to go and tries to talk us out of it, but we insist on going with Daddy. He paints a picture of a perfect little family living in a perfect little town, and it sounds so good to us.

We are currently living in a three-bedroom house with four adults and seven children, and there is constant arguing and chaos. The adults are usually drinking alcohol, and there is never enough money. The life Daddy describes seems like heaven to us.

Daddy packs our belongings into his car, and we travel across the country to go live with him in Marysville, Washington. Our oldest sister and her husband live in that area.

It is nice spending Halloween and Christmas with them, and so is living in the rental trailer that belongs to the parents of our brother-in-law. We try adjusting to our new environment and of being away from Momma.

Washington is a lot different than Louisiana. Mountain ranges replace the flat terrain we are used to. It is our first time seeing snow, and there is plenty of it. The colder temperatures warrant new coats for all of us.

The biggest difference between Louisiana and Washington is the people. We are accustomed to a more relaxed environment, and here everyone seems so formal. We feel as though the people here are better than us. We don't seem to fit in no matter how hard we try, and we miss Momma terribly. It's easy to take people out of the south, but it is hard to take the south out of the people.

After what seems like an eternity, Momma comes to join us in Washington. It appears that Daddy and Momma are trying to get along, because neither of them is drinking, but after only a few months Momma tells us she is secretly saving money to bring the three of us back to Houma with her. We are overjoyed because even though Momma is with us now, we still don't feel like we belong here. We love the schools, but we just don't fit in with the people.

We keep Momma's secret, but later it is revealed when we surprise Momma and buy her a trunk to put her clothes in for the trip.

Daddy knows something is up, so we have to leave sooner than Momma had planned. One day while Daddy is at work, the three of us get on a bus with Momma and travel back to Louisiana.

We are glad to be back in Houma. Momma rents a house on Engeron Street. We live here for a couple of months. Then we are evicted because Momma can't pay the rent. We have to sneak out of the house during the middle of the night. Most of our belongings, including all of our childhood photos, are left behind.

We have lived in five different houses, four towns and three states within this one year.

Chapter 4

Ghost Encounters

Linda is eleven years old, I am nine, and Joe is seven in 1968 when we get uprooted again and move to the little town of Klondike. It is down the bayou from Houma.

Jonnie is out of the Navy and lives with us. Our parents are still separated, and Daddy moves in with a woman across the bayou from us. We try to live a peaceful life, but it doesn't last long.

The house we rent is in a serene country setting, and a bayou is across the street from it. I like living here, and being by the water has its charms. It is relaxing to sit on the front porch and watch the shrimp boats with their nets raised high casually float by. Though our lives are unstable, we have many happy childhood moments.

Shrimp boats on the bayou.

Swimming in the bayou is a fun pastime and gives us relief from the stifling high temperatures and humidity here in the South. We also like to watch the crabs swim with their flippers going a hundred miles an hour. The critters nip at our feet as we try to avoid them, and they pinch our fingers when we try to catch them. The crabs' claws go up in a defensive position, and they wallop a nasty pinch. We soon learn to stay away from them.

Love bugs are plentiful, and they are easy to catch. They tickle while landing or crawling on your skin. They are called love bugs because two bugs become attached to each other during mating. Together they are about an inch long.

Another one of my favorites is lightning bugs. I am amazed that this small bug can light up the night sky, or at least their butt, as they try to attract a mate.

Chasing after them gives us something to do outdoors late in the evening. Momma supplies us with jars to catch the bugs in so we can have a closer look at them. Then we have fun releasing them and watching them fly away.

Uncle James and his family visit us often. We eat watermelons in the back yard and take turns churning homemade ice cream on the front porch. Sugar cane grows plentiful in this area, and we like the taste of it as we chew on the stalks to squeeze the sweet juice from them.

Cajun people speaking with broken French are common here. They are friendly folks. I like to hear them talk, especially when they greet everyone in a special way by saying things like, "Hey, dawlin'..." or "How ya doin', honey?" when they don't even know you.

We are used to this area because we pass through here almost every weekend on our way to and from the camp Momma's boyfriend owns, further down the bayou.

Houses are on both sides of us, but the large lots cause them to be spread out. This is common in Cajun Land.

Old wooden rocking chairs in the living room add to the relaxed atmosphere of the house, and these are part of the furnished rental. Living here is just what we need to calm our hectic lives—so it would seem.

Swamped by Ghosts

We aren't living in the house long when I start having the strange feeling that someone is watching us when we play outside. Sometimes I have a similar feeling while in the house. It seems different than just a kid's imagination at work. My family also notices the eerie atmosphere pervading the place, and they make comments about it.

Then something else strange happens. We are sitting in the rocking chairs in the living room one evening while watching television. All of a sudden an empty rocker starts rocking by itself! We are shocked and jump from our chairs to watch the unusual phenomena from the other side of the room.

We wonder if it is a ghost—and if so, if it is the spirit of Mrs. Trosclair. She died in the house before we moved into it.

There is no logical explanation for the chair to be rocking. There is no central cooling unit in the house. The fans are turned off, and all of the doors and windows are closed. The rocking chairs don't even move like this when the fans are on and the doors and windows are open.

Time passes, and once in a while that same chair rocks by itself. We are not as alarmed as when we first saw it, but none of us sit in that rocker anymore. It becomes known as Mrs. Trosclair's rocking chair.

Around this time another unusual thing occurs. We begin seeing a long-haired calico cat in our yard, and sometimes it is seen in our home. The peculiar thing about it is that none of us let the cat in the house. The mysterious cat looks real as it suddenly appears in one of the rooms and casually walks around in the house like it owns the place. No one opens the door to let the mysterious cat out of the house, but the cat is found outside later in the day.

The cat tries to attack us when we attempt to pet it, so we learn to leave it alone. We get used to the cat being around, and we name it Mrs. Trosclair.

We wonder if Mrs. Trosclair's spirit is somehow able to transform into the form of a cat, or if the cat belonged to Mrs. Trosclair when she was alive. The cat may have died, and maybe it now haunts the house with Mrs. Trosclair.

Something else begins to happen that baffles us. Underwear of all three of us females begins to disappear from our drawers, the clothes line, and from the laundry room. Momma buys us new ones, and those come up missing as well.

I am wondering if the ghost is taking them, but I'm puzzled as to what a ghost would do with underwear.

The washing machine couldn't have "eaten" the underwear. It would have also taken socks or our younger brother's underwear. We haven't noticed anything else missing from our home, that we know of.

The uneasy feeling in the house heightens, and something happens that frightens Momma. She sleeps alone in her bedroom, but she takes up only half of the large double bed. She usually lies on her side and faces the edge of the bed.

One night after settling into bed, Momma suddenly feels a freezing cold hand being placed upon her side! She looks around and doesn't see anyone in the room, but she feels an eerie presence in there.

Momma is terrified and isn't sure how to deal with this unusual phenomena. She decides to ignore the invisible specter, and soon it leaves.

Once in a while Momma can feel the cold unseen hand touch her side while in her bed. Sometimes she is afraid to sleep in her room alone, so Linda sleeps with her during those nights.

Linda climbs into bed with Momma one night and isn't there long when she feels the freezing cold hand being placed upon her side! It frightens Linda, and she tells Momma about it. They stay awake for a while to see if anything else unusual happens. Nothing does, on this night.

We are tired of moving, and we put up with the ghostly manifestations in order to continue living here.

I wonder if the cold hand that touched Momma and Linda belongs to the ghost of Mrs. Trosclair, and if our landlord moved out of the house because he felt the same cold touch of his deceased wife's hand upon him. It may have frightened him, too.

The large canopy bed in Momma's bedroom is part of the furnished house we rent. Mrs. Trosclair most likely died in this same bed.

Many years ago, the bed was probably draped with a sheer material to protect the owners against mosquitoes that come in droves in this area during the summer months.

(We never thought of asking the landlord about the unusual events happening in the house. He probably would have been too embarrassed to talk about the subject of the paranormal. It seemed too personal of a subject to bring up. Later I regretted not talking to him about it. He may have been able to shed some light on the mysterious things that were happening.)

Sometimes those who experience a ghostly presence feel the temperature in the room drop or feel a cold touch upon them. I wonder if the ghost touched Momma and Linda to try and scare them away, in order to touch the living, or to get them to move over. The departed soul may think it is still her bed and wants to get in it.

Mrs. Trosclair may also think Momma and Linda are intruders in her private quarters. She doesn't seem to mind us being in the living room, unless she rocked the chair to try and frighten us away.

There are many reasons for hauntings. Earth-bound spirits of the deceased seem to haunt sites of fateful events such as battles, murders, accidents, or suicides. Unsolved mysteries and untimely deaths seem to cause those spirits to be stuck in and haunt the area where their death occurred. Over and over they re-enact familiar behaviors or events that occurred when they were alive.

Some hauntings may occur because of unfinished business they had while still alive or because they did not want to leave loved ones behind. Mrs. Trosclair probably died of natural causes, and she seems to fit into one of these two categories.

True ghost stories like the ones mentioned throughout this book are vast, and they vary according to the situation. Sometimes people encounter ghosts while visiting a place that happens to be haunted. Others realize a house is haunted after they move into it.

Often people have pleasant encounters with the ghost of a person they knew when they were alive. Almost everyone who has had this kind of experience says it was comforting and helped to bring healing after the painful loss of that deceased person.

Some of the encounters occur right after the person dies, while others experience them weeks, months, or years later. Most of these situations are characterized as chance encounters. The people usually aren't seeking to communicate with the dead. Neither are psychics or other God-forbidden methods used.

The Bible doesn't mention much about ghosts, but the term was known at the time Jesus was living on the earth. Jesus suddenly appeared to his eleven disciples and other followers after his resurrection. The whole group was terrified when they saw Jesus, and they thought he was a ghost. Jesus told them to look at his hands and feet (his wounds) so they would know that it was him. He said for them to touch him and see that he wasn't a ghost—that a ghost wouldn't have flesh and blood like he had (Luke 24:36-39).

Immediately after Jesus had miraculously fed a multitude of well over five thousand people, he told his disciples to get into their boat and go to the other side of the lake while he sent the multitude away. Then Jesus went up into a mountain to pray alone. Nighttime came, and strong winds caused the disciples' boat to be tossed about in the high waves. About four o'clock that morning, Jesus walked on the water as he came out to them. When the disciples saw him, they screamed with fright because they thought he was a ghost. Jesus immediately told them not to be afraid—that it was him (Matthew 14:22-27).

These two stories in the Bible seem to indicate that there is such a thing as ghosts. Twice the disciples thought Jesus was a ghost when he appeared to them.

Jesus didn't mention the word "ghost" in his teachings, nor did he correct his disciples for using the word.

Many Christians believe that ghosts are actually demons in disguise. We can only speculate and form opinions on this subject.

No one knows for certain, but we should be open minded about the possibility of the existence of ghosts as we take a closer look at the supernatural events taking place all over the world.

God is the ultimate ruler of heaven and earth. Satan has control of the earth and the air surrounding it to a much lesser degree. He also has control over every deceased soul who doesn't serve God. Satan may be able to keep some of those lost souls bound on earth. A number of them may be forced to relive past experiences over and over.

A SPIRIT FOLLOWS US

It is getting dark outside as we drive home from a weekend at the camp further down the bayou. It is a nice getaway place that we go to once in a while. All of the windows in the car are down, and a fresh breeze brushes my face.

Linda is sitting in the front seat of our paneled station wagon with Momma. Joe and I are sitting by the back window, with our backs against the back seat—but not for long.

I am looking at the final hint of a sunset, when I glance to the left of me and see a solid, human-looking spirit following us! I am paralyzed with fright as it flies headfirst right behind the passenger side of the car where I am sitting. The spirit stays at the same speed we are going. It seems determined in its pursuit.

A few seconds later Joe sees it, too, and yells, "A ghost!" The quickness of Joe's words jerk me out of my panicked state, and both of us accidently hit each other as we scramble to turn around and climb into the back seat and away from its terrifying presence.

Momma asks, "Where?" She watches as Linda looks in the passenger side mirror and says, "There it is." Momma glances in the rear view mirror and becomes afraid when she sees it.

All of us frantically roll the windows up. We know that it won't keep the spirit from getting in, but it makes us feel safer.

Then the spirit hovers a little higher as if it is trying to hide from us. It seems to have been trying to sneak up on us but lost its element of surprise when we became aware of it.

Momma steps on the gas as she speeds down the dark, deserted, bayou road. We look back again and see that the spirit is gone. Apprehensively, I look around to make sure the impending spirit isn't near any of us. I am relieved to see that it is not.

We don't know how long the spirit was there before we noticed it behind us. It is terrifying to know that I was within its reach. The spirit could have grabbed me at any moment and pulled me out of the open window of the moving vehicle.

It seems strange to be glad that we are on our way back to the safety of our haunted house. As we near home, I am wondering if we lost the spirit or if it is hovering above the car or somewhere else where we can't see it.

We don't see the spirit when we exit the car, but we quickly go inside where we feel secure—for now.

The specter may have lost interest in us and started following the car that drove past us from the opposite direction. If it is a ghost, it may have a certain territory where it haunts, and it may have lost its opportunity to get us, this time.

I don't enjoy sitting in back of our station wagon after this frightening experience. The peaceful rides to the camp are now tainted with fear as I wonder if the spirit will re-emerge at any time along the way.

Many joys of our youth are shattered by unexpected trouble from the physical world we live in and from the spiritual world around us. We are being swamped by ghosts. They are haunting us in our home and outside of it. There seems to be no safe place for us.

We are also haunted by the traumatic events our family has had and by the uncertainty of what may happen next. But through it all, each new day brings with it the hope that things will be better.

WE BARELY ESCAPE

We are still living in Mr. Trosclair's house when something else unexpected and frightening happens. Linda and I take a bath together one evening, as little girls often do. We put lots of bubbles in the tub and climb into it. As the tub fills up with water, bubbles roll over the side and cascade onto the floor like a waterfall. We giggle with delight as we watch it.

Soon the floor by the tub disappears as bubbles cover it. I am the first one to finish bathing. There is no rug on the floor as I step out of the tub, and I slip on the many bubbles gathered at my feet. The floor slants at a sharp angle toward the back door. This causes me to slide all the way across the long room. I land with a thump against the back door.

Both of us are quiet for a few seconds from the shock of what is happening, and to make sure I am not hurt. Then my sister and I burst out laughing because it looked so funny.

Soon it is Linda's turn to get out of the tub. Very carefully she steps onto the floor, but she loses her footing and comes sliding into me as I make my way back to the tub to get my towel. Both of us crash into the door. We squeal with laughter because it is so much fun.

We have created a Cajun slip-n-slide. Each time we almost make it to the towel holder, we slip and find ourselves back at the door, giggling the whole while.

Both of us playfully yell "Help!" as we make a game out of it and wash the floor at the same time. Momma doesn't see it that way later when she discovers the mess we make.

We are getting tired after a while of doing this. Then Linda almost makes it to the tub, and she glances back at me as I slip and slide past her. She suddenly screams and points to the back door.

We are terrified as we watch a man's hairy arm slide through the crack of the chained back door! He is trying to take the security chain off of the door. There is nothing I can do to avoid sliding within his reach. Our fun game is now turning into a horrible nightmare.

I wonder if the man was watching us this whole time, waiting for the opportune moment to grab one or both of us. I panic and wonder what the man will do to us if he gets the chain off of the door. It is the only thing between us and him.

We scream for help, but our screams go unnoticed because we have been screaming playfully for a while.

When my feet slam into the wall near the back door, the man grabs my right ankle and tries to hold on to it—but my leg is so full of soap that he can't hold it for long. I immediately pull my leg back, only to have him grab my other one.

I start kicking his arm as Linda comes crashing into the door. The weight of her body against the door and the force of my frantic kicks cause the man to retrieve his arm out of the door.

Linda quickly locks the door, and we work our way to the other bathroom door. We grab towels from the closet along the way and wrap them around us as we run out of the room.

We tell Momma what happened. She turns the back porch light on and looks for the man through the window of the locked kitchen door. He is not on the screened-in back porch that leads to the kitchen and bathroom.

Then we trail close behind Momma, as she goes into the bathroom to see if the door is still locked and to get our clothes from in there. Momma gets angry when she sees the soap everywhere. She puts towels on the wet floor and fusses us for making the mess.

Our aunt and her four children come to visit us the next day. They park their pickup truck next to our car, which is by the screened-in back porch.

We go outside to greet them. Our mother and aunt have a look around and discover marks on the old water cistern behind the bathroom, indicating that someone has climbed up and into it. They also see a ladder that is not ours sitting up against the bathroom window.

The man probably climbed the ladder and watched us through the window as we took our bath. This perverted man is probably the one who took our underwear. He may have come into the house while we were gone.

Our parents are still separated, and we have not fully recovered from being traumatized not long ago by a murderer that hid in our upstairs apartment for two weeks.

We have had to move several times in a short period of time, and right as we begin to relax and feel safe in this house, we realize it is haunted. Now we have to deal with the physical threats of this traumatic event.

Our emotions have been like a roller coaster from one traumatic event to the other—as well as from an already hectic life of growing up in an alcoholic, dysfunctional home. Now our personal security is in question, and we feel vulnerable in our own home.

This sexual predator was influenced by evil spirits and harbored evil thoughts. I shudder to think what he may have tried to do to us.

The bubbles we were playing in probably saved our lives, because the man couldn't hold onto me or get the chain off of the door when Linda slid into it. We narrowly escaped the clutches of this evil man, but it isn't the last time we encounter him.

All of us are standing near the two automobiles while our mother and aunt discuss what to do about the situation. Suddenly, our aunt yells, "I see the man! He's by the cistern!"

This frightens all of us and makes us even more afraid, because when she says he's by the cistern (water reservoir), we think she is saying that he's by Sister (or Sissy), which is her only daughter's nick name.

Momma yells to us, "Get in the car!" All of us take off running to the two automobiles. Most of us kids jump into the back of our aunt's pickup truck, because it is easier to get into.

Our mother and aunt quickly start the automobiles, and tires screech as they take off down the road.

This is not the same man that was in the attic of our upstairs apartment. He was of a different nationality.

We have been living in this house for only a few months. Momma begins looking for another house to rent. We can't seem to settle down anywhere. Something always happens that causes us to relocate. It is hard for us, but it must also be hard for Momma.

Chapter 5

Knock, Knock, Who's There?

Linda is eleven years old, I am nine, and Joe is seven in 1968 when we move out of Mr. Trosclair's house and into a rental with Uncle James and his large family on Pontiff Street in Houma. (They moved around about as much as we did.)

No unusual things happen while living here, unless they go unnoticed because of the noise level and busy activities of the many people in the house.

When I turn almost eleven years old, Daddy and Momma get back together again. We move out of Uncle James's house and into a two bedroom rental on St. Peter Street. It is in the same neighborhood. Things return to normal for a while—or what seems normal to us.

Momma in 1970.

Our mother is the center of our lives and is talented in many ways. We enjoy spending time with her as she teaches us how to sew, crochet, and do craft projects.

Momma sews some of our clothes and makes curtains for the windows. Once she even re-upholsters the furniture. She does most of the maintenance on our automobile herself, which includes changing the spark plugs. I am intrigued as I watch her. She usually fixes our car when it breaks down, because she can't rely on Daddy to do it. I learn how handy a hammer can be.

One night Daddy doesn't return home at a reasonable time from a romp at the local bar. Momma leaves to go get him and to bring her very-drunk-by-now husband home.

Linda's friend from next door is visiting, and they decide to play with the Ouija board. Linda pulls the game out of our bedroom closet, and the girls sit on the floor near the two double beds.

I am nervous that they are playing the eerie game while our parents aren't home, but I'm not too alarmed, because I have seen the girls play it at other times and nothing scary happened.

They laugh and have a good time as they play with it. I am afraid of the game and stay away from it. I know something unseen is controlling it, and that it is not God.

Linda and her friend ask the board questions, and the board answers them by mysteriously moving the planchette, or triangle-shaped plastic piece of the game, to letters on the board as the girls' fingertips lightly touch it.

The girls are unaware that they are actually conjuring up an evil spirit, and that spirit is now in our home. It is a demon that they are asking questions of, and the demon is moving the planchette to answer the questions.

Linda and her friend decide to do something different. They remove their fingertips from the planchette and sit with their hands in their lap as they ask the board questions. Then the Ouija board does something unexpected. The planchette moves by itself across the board as it answers every question Linda and her friend ask.

This is freaking me out as I watch in dismay. The girls are amused by it, until they become frightened when the entity spells out a threatening message that it is coming to get Linda's friend at midnight!

I am walking through the short hall by the bedroom door when I hear them read aloud what the board says, and I, too, become afraid.

The two girls jump up, and all three of us run into the living room where Joe is. Joe becomes involved in the conversation as all of us anxiously wait in the living room for our parents to return. Being alone in the house late at night causes us to be even more frightened.

Momma stays in the bar for quite a while as she tries to coax Daddy into coming home with her. Both of them are drinking this whole time.

The house is quiet, and we are on edge as we watch the clock strike midnight. All of a sudden, we hear noises in the carport! Then the kitchen doorknob jiggles as if someone is trying to open the door.

My heart beats fast as I anxiously wait to see what will happen next. Abrupt banging on the kitchen door causes us to scream in unison, and jumping from fright almost sends us through the ceiling.

We huddle together on the couch, and with dread I am thinking, *Oh no! The spirit is coming to get us!* I am sure the others are thinking the same thing. All eyes are staring at the kitchen door, when suddenly the knob turns and the door slowly opens!

I almost faint with fright—until I hear Daddy's angry voice as he complains to Momma that he couldn't get the door open. He was so drunk that he couldn't get the key in the hole. Momma had to unlock the door for him.

Linda and her friend are so afraid of the Ouija board that they never play with it again. Linda doesn't get rid of it, though. It just gets stuffed behind all of the other games in our closet.

This experience frightens me so much that I have trouble sleeping for a while. I stay awake each night waiting to see if an evil entity will invade our home, or wondering if is it already here.

This experience and other traumatic events in our lives are probably why the three of us have such a close bond. Sometimes all we have is each other for support. It may also be why we are sensitive to the spiritual things that are happening around us.

Later I learn that the Ouija board is a part of the black arts and should be avoided at all costs. You can't play games with evil spirits, and you can't play games with God. Stay away from evil things and turn to God instead. He knows your future, and He has plans to bless you.

Children play with these sorts of things thinking they are just games. They don't realize what they are doing in the spirit realm. What seems like an innocent game may open spiritual doors in the dark world and invite demons into their homes and lives. The Spirit of Witchcraft and other evil spirits are associated with these kinds of practices.

Some people who practice witchcraft and dabble in the occult think they are controlling the demons and telling them what to do, but in reality they are the ones being controlled by Satan and the demons.

Jesus can set people free from all spiritual bondages, no matter how far they have gone. Serving God is so much better, and having peace with God cannot compare to anything the devil may offer.

1 Thessalonians 5:22-23 states, "Abstain from all appearance of evil. And the very God of peace sanctify you wholly; and I pray God your whole spirit and soul and body be preserved blameless unto the coming of our Lord Jesus Christ."

All of us in the house have done things we shouldn't. These sins may also be opening spiritual doors for demonic forces to enter our home and lives.

There is a war going on in the spiritual realm. God and his army are fighting against Satan and his evil cohorts. This war also affects the physical world in which we live. But God's side of the battle has two-thirds more angelic warriors than the evil side, and God wins in the end. He is more powerful than any evil force.

Linda is thirteen years old, I am eleven, and Joe is nine in 1970 when our parents split up again. We move with Uncle James and his family to Beatrice Street in Houma.

Soon, with parental permission, Linda gets married. She moves out, but she and her husband come to visit us often.

In 1971, Uncle James and his family move with us to St. Pius Street, which is in the same neighborhood we had been living.

One day Linda, her best friend, and my best friend come to visit us. The two girls are sisters. Linda and her friend decide to do a séance to try and communicate with the spirit of a loved one of theirs who recently died. This is the friend who played the Ouija board with Linda when we lived next door to them.

Four of our cousins want to participate, and they join us as we sit in a circle on the double bed. A few of them are skeptical, and they laugh as they make fun of the whole ordeal.

I am a little skeptical myself, but I am also curious to know if this method of communication with the dead actually works.

The spirit of Mrs. Trosclair seemed to be trying to communicate with us when she sat in the rocking chair and touched Momma on her side when we lived in her house. If she spoke to us, we were not able to hear her.

We settle down and get quiet as the séance begins. My curiosity peaks as someone tries to conjure up a spirit. A few minutes later, Linda's friend begins to go into a trance-like state as she closes her eyes and behaves in a strange way.

We can tell she isn't faking it, and we know that she isn't the sort of person to do that. She certainly didn't want to be the one to be used as a medium. Almost everyone involved in the séance becomes afraid and simultaneously jumps off of the bed.

The spell on the girl begins to be broken, and she slumps over as if unconscious or dead. This frightens us even more. Then the girl falls over and gets wedged between the wall and the bed.

Linda and the girl's sister (my best friend), who were sitting next to her, help the girl back onto the bed. She gradually comes to and is not aware of what has happened. This ordeal scares us, and we never try to have a séance again.

These sorts of things are treated as entertainment by many people. Some like to make fun of the experience, like our cousins did. Others, like us, are curious about the unseen spiritual world.

No matter the reason, these things should not be taken lightly. They should be avoided.

Toward the end of the year, Linda becomes mother to a remarkable baby boy, James. We call him Jamie.

I am thirteen years old and Joe is eleven in 1972 when Uncle James's family and ours decide to separate. We move into a small house on Slater Street, which is across town. Linda and her family move there with us.

Momma sleeps in the lower bunk bed in our bedroom and Joe on the top one. I sleep on the floor in front of the dresser. Linda's family takes up residence in the other bedroom.

Toys and games are neatly placed on the shelves in our bedroom closet, along with Linda's Ouija board.

I get rid of all of my dolls except my favorite one. She is tall and can walk with assistance and batteries. I have outgrown the doll and don't play with her anymore, but I am not ready to part with her yet. I take the dead batteries out of the doll and gently place her on a shelf in the closet. My younger cousin wants the doll and knows I will give it to her soon.

We aren't living here long when we begin sensing an eerie presence in the house. We are aware of these kinds of things because of what we have already been through, and living with Daddy has taught us to be sensitive to things around us. We watch him closely to see what mood he is in when he is home.

Then we begin hearing what sounds like someone snoring in our bedroom wall, near the bunk beds! The house next door is too far away for us to hear snoring from there.

Spirits usually make themselves known to unwary humans by knocking or banging on walls and doors, but this is the first time I have heard of this type of manifestation. This odd snoring sound always occurs in the same place in the wall, and it is located only a few feet from where I sleep. My head almost touches that area of the wall.

The snoring is sporadic and occurs during the day and at night. The strange sounds don't seem threatening, but a pervading evil presence fills the room when it is taking place. It is unsettling and unnerving. It is also creepy knowing that something alive is causing the noise.

I am apprehensive each night when I go to bed, as I wonder what the spirit may do next. It takes a while for me to fall asleep when the snoring is active.

Friends and neighbors come over to witness the unusual phenomena in our home. My best friend from our old neighborhood, who did the séance with us, is among them. She apprehensively enters our bedroom and hears the snoring. It frightens her so much that she urinates on herself.

News of our haunted house spreads around town like a wild fire and comes to the attention of the local TV station. They interview Momma, record the phenomena, and publicize the paranormal activity. Soon what seems like an endless line of people are at our front door and across our front yard. They enter our home and bedroom one at a time to witness the unusual event.

We are not happy about the attention placed upon our family or the inconvenience of constantly having strangers enter the privacy of our home. Gradually the curiosity of outsiders subsides, and we have peace—but not for long.

Other unusual things begin to happen in the house. We only tell a few people about them, because we don't want another bombardment of the whole town in our home again.

The snoring in the wall begins to escalate. It is around this time that I attend a church revival in the neighborhood. I see healing miracles take place during the services, and I learn about how to become a born-again believer in Christ Jesus. My heart yearns to convert to Christianity, but I am afraid to go to the altar by myself to pray. After the service ends and it is time to leave, I immediately regret not taking the opportunity to go up to the altar.

During the next two days, a few traumatic incidents occur that cause me to deliberately seek God, realizing I don't need to be in a church to do this. I slip into Linda's empty bedroom so I can be alone with God. Lying face down on the floor, I say a simple prayer as I ask for His forgiveness. With tears rolling down my cheeks, I ask God to come into my life.

The strange snoring sounds in the wall get louder and louder as time goes by. Now it sounds threatening, and it sends goose bumps down my spine. I pray fervently for God to protect us.

About a week later I begin noticing something strange happening when I play the small organ that is in our bedroom. I play different types of songs on the organ, but my favorite is gospel music. I worship God as I listen to the words of the songs while singing and playing them.

The organ begins turning off by itself only when I play Christian music on it. There is a click sound, and I see the knob turn to the off position.

I turn the organ back on, and it stays on while I play any other type of music. Then the organ turns off by itself again when I begin playing a gospel song on it.

Soon another spirit manifestation occurs in our home, and it frightens all of us. While walking into our bedroom from school one day, I notice that my doll is lying on the top bunk in our bedroom. As I gently place it back in the closet, I am wondering why someone took the doll out of there.

I question my family about it, and I am told that no one touched the doll. It is puzzling, but I don't think much about it.

While Joe and I are at school the next day, Linda goes to get something out of our bedroom closet and is shocked to see my doll's head turn on its own and face her! She quickly leaves the bedroom and goes to tell Momma about it.

I don't know any of this when I get home from school, but I sense a strong evil presence in our bedroom as I walk in there to put my school bag away. I have the feeling that someone is watching me. Goose bumps rise up on the nape of my neck as I get near the bunk beds.

Then I notice that my doll is lying on the top bunk again, and it is face up like it was before. Suddenly dread rises up in me as the doll's head slowly turns by itself and faces me!

The doll seems alive, and it is as if someone is looking at me instead of just a doll facing me. At this moment, I realize the doll is possessed with an evil spirit.

Horrified, I slowly turn around to leave the room—fearing that the spirit may attack me if I make a sudden move. Not wanting to look at the creepy doll, but afraid not to, I continue watching as the doll's head turns and follows my every move as I walk past it. Once in the hallway, I run to tell Momma about it.

She informs me about the experience Linda had with the doll. I am terrified and don't want to go back into our room or touch the doll again.

Then Momma does something unexpected. She puts the doll back in the closet and says that she will get rid of it tomorrow. Those words seem like eternity to me. I want the doll gone immediately. I fear that something dreadful may happen between now and tomorrow.

Apprehensive and full of fear as bedtime draws near, I am dreading having to go into that closet to get my bed roll. I am not afraid of the doll as much as I am of the entity that is controlling it.

I don't know what to expect as I open the closet door. I sense that the spirit is powerful and hope it is not going to jump on me when I enter the closet.

Carefully reaching for my bedding, I am almost surprised that nothing sinister happens. Nevertheless, I quickly close the door and settle on the floor in front of the dresser. The closet is near my feet.

I am lying on my back and my eyes are fixated on the closet door, as I wonder if the possessed doll will come out of the closet and attack me during the night. Another spirit is making snoring sounds by my head. I am surrounded by evil and am beside myself with anxiety, as I anticipate that something may happen at any time.

Suddenly louder snoring in the wall invades my thoughts. Just about this time Momma does something that scares me even more. She gets her Bible and sits on the bottom bunk bed. Then she randomly opens the Bible and places it on her lap. Momma lays her hand on the open pages as she begins talking to the spirit that is in the wall!

I am freaking out and about to ask her to stop when she demands the spirit to show itself. I am thinking, *Oh no! This is not good!*

The snoring immediately stops. All four of us nervously look around the room for any signs of the entity appearing before us. I am still lying on my back, when suddenly the evil spirit jumps on top of me! I can't see it, but I know it is there.

The spirit is strong as it holds me down, but it feels different than if a human would attack me. It is more of a paralyzing feeling than a weight on me, and there is a slight tingling sensation similar to goose bumps or a light electrical current. It is like when your leg falls asleep, but the feeling is all over your body. The pressure is not painful, but it is frightening not being able to move.

I yell, "It's on top of me!" I want to scream for help, but I know there is nothing my family can do to free me from this malicious spirit.

My fear intensifies when all of a sudden what feels like two large hands start strangling me! I'm not sure if it is the same spirit or a different one. I panic and try to scream, but only a strange sound comes out of my vocal chords.

Thinking I am going to die when the grip on my throat gets tighter, I decide to ask Jesus for help. No sound comes from my constricted throat when I try to call out his name.

This demon is trying to kill me and I need help right away, but I know that no human can assist me in this situation. I am wondering if Jesus can hear me as I call out to him silently in my mind.

The demon seems to have a lot of rage toward me—and even more toward Jesus, whom I am summoning to help me. I become even more frightened when I hear Linda say that my face is turning blue.

Summoning up my newfound faith, I say the name of Jesus stronger this time. There is still no sound coming from my vocal chords, but the demon loosens its grip on my throat a little. My prayers are working!

I say the name of Jesus again, and this time I can hear myself whisper. The invisible hands on my neck loosen even more. When I say the name of Jesus once more, my voice is loud. The demon lets out an ear-piercing scream, releases its death grip on my throat, and jumps off of me.

I begin to cough, and my throat hurts. Linda says that my neck is red, and my family sees a set of large fingerprints on my throat. I am in awe to see that Jesus kicked the demon's butt, and it increases my faith in Him.

Ephesians 6:10-12 states, "Finally my brethren, be strong in the Lord, and in the power of his might. Put on the whole armour of God, that you may be able to stand against the wiles of the devil. For we wrestle not against flesh and blood, but against principalities, against powers, against the rulers of the darkness of this world, against spiritual wickedness in high places."

The doll doesn't come out of the closet anymore after this, but I still don't like it anywhere around me. I give the doll to my cousin.

A few weeks later we go to visit them. As we pull into their driveway, I notice only the head of the doll lying in the ditch. The face of the doll happens to be facing me, but I am not afraid of it. I never thought that I would ever say that I am glad my favorite doll was torn to pieces by my male cousins.

Linda doesn't play with her Ouija board anymore, but she does still read people's fortunes by using the Bible. She is good at it. Momma does it, too, but she isn't as accomplished as Linda.

They don't realize that what they are doing is a type of white witching or soothsaying, which the Word of God advises to stay away from.

All of us have been doing things we shouldn't. These things may be opening doors in the spiritual realm and allowing evil spirits to enter our home. The Bible says to not give in to the temptations of sin.

The devil is behind all sinful thoughts and actions. He is waiting for you to mess up your life. If you give him an inch, he will take a mile. Sin will always cost you more than you are willing to pay.

Satan's major areas of destruction in people's lives are physical sickness, family problems, financial problems, mental and emotional attacks, and bondage, especially to alcohol, drugs, and sex.

Satan affects people by using demons of his spirit army. People may be dealing with more than one spirit. Demons can team up, but one is usually more dominant

Jesus came to destroy the works of the devil. Most of Jesus's ministry was in doing spiritual battle. One-third of his ministry was in casting out demons. This shows how important it is. There's power in the name of Jesus. There is power in his blood. It cleanses us of sin and sets us free from Satan's grip. There is power in the Holy Spirit. He convicts us of sin and leads us to the truth.

Luke 8:2 tells of Jesus setting Mary Magdalene free of seven demons. She was a prostitute and invited those evil spirits into her life by her sinful actions.

The demonic activity in our home may have something to do with my age. Sometimes this happens in a house where a preteen girl or boy lives, but most of the time it is a girl who experiences this.

It could be the age of spiritual accountability, when preteens are presented with the choice to serve God or not. My desire to serve God may have provoked the evil spirits to manifest themselves. The demons may have been angry that they lost control over me. Evil spirits probably view me as the enemy now. I represent a threat to them by bringing God into my life and into our home. They know that they may be forced to leave.

A LIVING DOLL

Years later, a friend of mine (who I will call Nancy) told me a chilling story of something that happened to her when she was twelve years old. It was similar to our doll experience, and she had the same type of doll I had at the age of twelve. There seems to be a supernatural connection with our two incidents. I wonder if Nancy and I had both done something that caused a demon to enter our dolls or if something happened during the manufacturing of the dolls that caused the dolls to be possessed.

Nancy and her sister were playing in their bedroom when a movement on the floor caught Kathy's attention. It was her doll. She noticed that the head of the doll was facing her. It was lying face up on its back when she put it down earlier. It also puzzled Nancy to see that the doll's eyes were open. Before this, the eyes were always closed when the doll was lying down.

Nancy suddenly felt that something wasn't right, and she sensed an evil presence in the room. She told her sister about it.

Both of the girls became afraid and began moving away from the doll. They freaked out when the head and eyes of the doll followed their every move! It was as if the doll had come alive.

The two girls screamed and ran out of the room. They told their parents about it.

Their parents thought the girls just had overactive imaginations, but they decided to go look at the doll in order to appease the girls, so they would calm down and not be afraid.

The kids followed their parents down the hall and crouched at the bedroom door while their father and mother stepped into the room. Their father stayed by the bedroom door while their mother walked over to the doll.

She wasn't paying attention to the doll as she looked at the children and dramatically thrust both open hands toward the doll, saying, "See? It is just a doll." But Nancy's mother knew something wasn't right when she saw fear in the children's faces. Mouths were open and eyes were wide as they stared at the doll. Her husband even looked scared.

She looked back at the doll as she slowly stepped away from it. She, too, became afraid when the doll's head turned to follow her every movement, as if the doll were alive. Realizing that the doll was possessed, Nancy's mother quickly grabbed it and threw it into the garbage can outside.

Everyone talked excitedly about the strange thing that had happened. When the family calmed down a little later, they could hear scraping sounds on the gutter pipe on the side of the house. Nancy's mother looked out of the window and was shocked to see the doll climbing up the pipe!

The possessed doll scooted inch by inch up the gutter pipe and toward the open window. Terror stricken, she quickly closed and locked the window.

The family wanted to witness this unbelievable scene and took turns glancing out of the window at the possessed doll. Then they scrambled to close and lock all of the other windows, while their father checked the doors to make sure they were locked.

The family huddled together in the living room and stayed up most of the night, watching and waiting to see if the doll would find a way to enter their home. The house remained quiet, and family members fell asleep one at a time.

Tension returned the next morning as the family nervously looked out of the windows for the impending doll. They didn't notice anything unusual, and it was quiet outside, but Nancy's mother remained apprehensive because she knew her husband would be leaving for work soon.

Their father cautiously opened the front door when he left. The family huddled behind him, but not too close in case the doll scurried into the house as soon as he opened the door.

After he stepped out of the house without any incidents, the rest of the family apprehensively looked out of the door. The doll was nowhere in sight. They didn't know where it went, but were glad it never returned to their home.

I know these stories sound unreal, but they are absolutely true. Over the years, I have heard other accounts of people who have had similar experiences with this particular doll. Those people also realized that the doll was demon possessed.

Demons can manifest as a spirit or in physical form. Some demons are assigned to certain areas where authority was given to them. Others may be limited to certain places such as a house or grave yard, or they may be assigned to an item, an animal, or a person.

They possess objects so they can get into homes and disturb people's lives. Demons possess humans in order to destroy them and to use them as living hosts to do their bidding. Many demons can reside in one person.

Satan and his demons hate all humans, and they are jealous of humankind because we are made in God's image and because God gives us mercy and grace.

A demon-possessed person can turn to God and repent. This will cancel the authority the demon has over him or her, and the demon must leave.

That person will be protected from evil forces as long as he or she serves God faithfully. But this person must be careful not to give place to the devil again. If he or she commits those same sins again, the demon may come back like a storm.

Satan is like a lion. He roams around to see whom he can devour (destroy), and he keeps a close eye on Christians. If you mess up, repent—and God will help you get back on the right track again.

1 Peter 5:8 says, "Be sober, be vigilant; because your adversary the devil, as a roaring lion, walketh about, seeking whom he may devour."

BATTERIES NOT INCLUDED

Years after my experience with the doll, I have a frightening encounter with another type of toy. It requires batteries, and it can talk when activated. The toy makes life-like movements as it speaks.

My job at the time requires me to go to a lady's home to take care of her grown daughter. One day, upon entering the home, I notice one of these popular toys sitting on the coffee table in the living room. I have seen this toy in stores, and I have sensed an evil presence while walking past the display.

I have heard fear-provoking, true accounts of this particular toy being possessed by evil spirits. A few friends of mine had such encounters with it. Hoping to never be in personal contact with one of them, now this toy is sitting in front of me as I sit on the couch, and its face is toward me.

The lady thinks I am interested in the toy when she sees me looking at it, and she turns the toy on to demonstrate what it does. It says the usual things a toy like that would say. Then she turns the toy off and returns it to the table.

I don't let the fearful thoughts bother me or distract me from doing my job. Out of the many toys like this one being sold, I hope there are only a small number of them to be concerned about.

The lady leaves the house to run errands. Her daughter and I are still sitting in the living room talking about what she would like to do today. Suddenly the doll begins to speak. I am wondering if the lady had accidently left the toy on.

I pick the toy up and see that the button is in the "off" position. A few minutes after putting the toy down, it speaks again. Wondering if the toy is broken, I flip the switch back and forth. It is in the "off" position when I place it back on the table.

I am not paying attention to the toy as I talk to the woman. Then I begin having the feeling that someone is watching me. An evil presence pervades the room, and the toy begins to talk as if it is speaking directly to me! My suspicion is confirmed when we hear the toy say things like, "Me no like you," and "I hate you."

It is talking completely different than when the woman turned the toy on earlier. At first, I disregard the rude comments. The woman looks puzzled and a little afraid.

Then it says other mean things. I tell the woman, "What strange things for a toy to say." She agrees with me and gets angry as she says, "Get rid of it!"

Feeling intimidated by the evil spirit that is controlling the toy, I take the batteries out of it and place them on the coffee table. A few minutes later the toy speaks again, but this time without the batteries in it!

I am looking at the batteries sitting on the table when the toy says in a deep sinister voice, "I'll get you." Goose bumps rise up on my neck. I try not to show fear as I pick up the possessed toy and put it on the top shelf of the woman's bedroom closet. I don't know what else to do with it.

A while later we go into the bedroom for something, and we hear the toy with no batteries talking from inside of the closet! The woman and I look at each other with fear, and I casually say, "Let's go somewhere." The woman agrees, and we leave the house in haste. Our destination is the movie theater.

We return to the house just as her mother drives up. The woman and I look at each other and don't say a word about the terrifying experience, because we know that her mother will probably not take us seriously.

The stories of these two toys remind me of the statue in Revelation 13 of the Bible. The statue comes to life, and people all over the world will worship it. The statue will even be able to speak, and it will order anyone who doesn't worship it to be killed. An evil spirit will possess the statue in the end days and make it appear to be alive. It is the same type of occurrence as seen in possessed toys and other items.

The statue in Revelation is also a parallel to the gold statue in Daniel 3 that King Nebuchadnezzar made. He set the statue up and commanded all of the people to worship it. Those who refused to worship it were killed by being thrown into a fiery furnace.

Evil spirits can enter certain objects. They can also be channeled through objects by occult practices. Spells and curses can be placed on objects to advance evil. Children can become susceptible and open to incantations that are placed on the items.

Not everything is as innocent as you think it is. Just seeing the grotesque features on some toys and other objects is evidence that they are not wholesome. Go through your closets. Clean out your homes. Get rid of things that are not of God. Pray about everything, and leave nothing to chance.

———————

Chapter 6

Spooked on St. Michelle Avenue

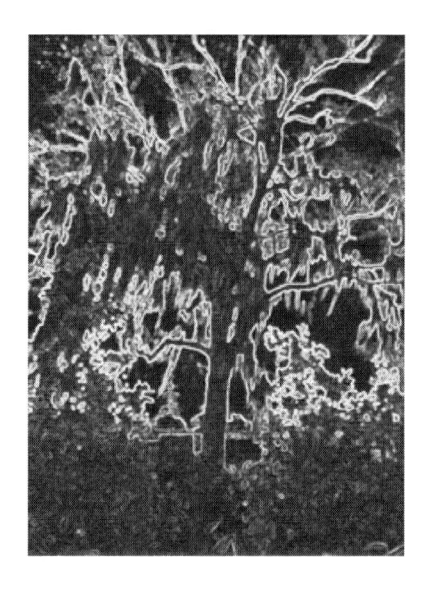

Linda and her husband divorce, and she and her son Jamie continue to live with us.

Linda is sixteen, I am fourteen, and Joe is twelve in 1973 when we move a few streets over to St. Michelle Avenue. Jonnie and his family of six move there with us.

It is a large, six-bedroom house that was three separate apartments before we moved into it. Jonnie's family lives in the front section of the house, and our family stays in the back of it. A door in the middle room separates the two living quarters, but it is always kept open.

Swamped by Ghosts

There are twelve of us sharing the living space, but there is plenty of room for all of us. We eat meals together, and we all hang out in the main rooms.

Jonnie and his wife Betty stay in the front bedroom. Their daughter Tina is in the bedroom near them. A full bath is between the two rooms. Eliot and their youngest son, Jonnie Jr., share a bedroom between Tina's room and our parents' large bedroom. Jonnie Jr. starts kindergarten while living here.

Linda and her son James sleep in our parents' large room. There's plenty of space for the two double beds in there—one bed for our parents and the other one Linda and James sleep in. A set of bunk beds are stacked against the wall for Joe and I to sleep in on the nights that Daddy works.

Joe's and my bedrooms are located at the back of the house, and a full bath is between them. Joe's room is adjoined to our parents' bedroom. My room is by the den.

Joe and I both sense an evil presence on the side of the house where our rooms are. It is similar to the evil presence we encountered in the house we just moved from, but without the snoring sounds we heard in the wall.

I wonder if the evil spirit followed us to our new residence. I hope not. My anxiety is heightened as I become keenly aware that I may be attacked again if it is that spirit.

Joe's room is dark and dungeon-like because there are no windows in there, but my bedroom is the creepiest room in the house. It is unnerving, but I try to remain positive. At least I have a room of my own.

Sometimes it suddenly gets unnaturally cold in my room, and at times it stays that way for hours. This happens even in the summer months.

Those who enter my room notice the temperature change and comment about it. We don't have a central air system in the house, a fan is not in my room, and the window is sealed shut for some reason. I always keep the two doors to my room closed. It is stuffy and hot in there most of the time.

Joe and I like having our own rooms to hang out in, but we are glad to sleep in our parents' bedroom on the nights when Daddy works.

I was told that the back part of the large house was a bar room at one time. This would make sense, because of the neon beer sign that hangs from the ceiling and the long, L-shaped bar that extends across what is now our den.

Our parents' room is large enough to house three or more pool tables, and I was told that it was the pool room.

My bedroom was supposedly used by the ladies of the night who entertained the men. The room has an eerie atmosphere about it. Once in a while I get the feeling that I am intruding in someone else's territory while in my room, and I sense that someone is watching my every move. These distractions affect me, and sometimes I have trouble concentrating on my schoolwork or going to sleep.

Another strange thing happens right after settling into the house. We always keep the windows in the kitchen closed, but I notice that they are open one day when I walk past them. The windows were closed when I passed by there a few minutes ago, and no one else has entered the room.

I tell Betty about it. She closes the windows, and she is puzzled about the incident. Once in a while the windows mysteriously open again.

I wonder if it is a ghost that is opening the windows, and if it is the cause of the other strange things that are happening in the house. I am not interested in ghosts and don't want them anywhere near me, yet I am repeatedly thrust into the strange world of the paranormal.

Linda remarries in June 1974, and the wedding takes place in our large house on St. Michelle Avenue. Linda looks beautiful as she walks down the den steps to join her new husband, Carroll Bourgeois.

Linda and Jamie.

Linda and Jamie move out of our house and into Carroll's trailer. A few months later they buy a house. Paranormal events begin to happen there. The spirit of a man and that of a young girl are often seen in their home. Those stories are told in detail in Chapter Eight of this book.

MIRROR MANIFESTATION

All of us are busy with our lives on St. Michelle Avenue. We don't talk much about the unusual things that are happening in the house.

Uncle James becomes a Christian, and I start going to church with him. I get serious about serving God, listen only to Christian music, and read my Bible daily.

I have many friends at school, but only a few close ones. Drew (whose name has been changed for reasons of privacy) is among those chosen few. I met him at the beginning of this school year.

We find out later that Drew's mother is bosom buddies with my mom. What a coincidence. My mother works for her, and their trailer sits on the property of the business.

School lets out for the summer, and I only get to see Drew a few brief times when I go with Momma to visit her friend.

One day Momma's friend informs her that Drew has died! He was only fifteen years old—the same age I am. I am told that he was accidentally shot by another child.

I am devastated by the tragedy, and I'm still upset when my cousin, Nora Jewell, comes over for a visit a few days after attending the funeral. Nora and Tina try to cheer me up as the three of us sit on top of the long bar in the den.

Swamped by Ghosts

Betty casually walks into the den from the front of the house, and the rest of the family is in different areas of the den, when our conversation abruptly stops. I suddenly feel compelled to go open the cabinet under the sink. An unusual sadness engulfs me as I jump down from the counter and slowly head to the sink.

Everyone in the room seems to be aware that something is amiss. They stop what they are doing and watch intensely as I reluctantly open the cabinet under the sink that houses our old newspapers. I don't know what to expect but sense that something is about to happen.

I don't pay attention to the date on the newspaper that I randomly select and pull out from the large stack. I sit cross-legged in the middle of the den floor and lay the newspaper in my lap. Everyone in the room gathers around as I casually open the newspaper to what happens to be the obituary section. Glancing at the first thing I see when I open the page, I gasp and say, "Look! It's Drew's obituary."

As soon as I say this, fresh red liquid that looks like blood suddenly appears on Drew's obituary! All of us gasp in unison as we witness the unusual phenomena. It appears to be blood from a fresh wound.

All of us watch in horror as it slowly spreads across the open page in front of me. There was not one drop of red liquid on the newspaper when I first opened it.

I scream and quickly toss the newspaper aside as I jump up from the floor to get away from it. I look at my hands to see if any of the blood got on them and am relieved when I see none.

Spooked on St. Michelle Avenue

The red liquid stopped spreading across the newspaper the moment I threw it down. Momma crumbles the newspaper up and throws it in the garbage can.

I wonder if my recently deceased friend is trying to tell me something, and voice this thought aloud. Nora and others in the room agree.

Then everyone remains strangely quiet. No one speaks, though one would expect them to. We are all at a loss for words, and we nervously look around the room as we continue watching to see what may happen next. Everyone knows about the boy's death and that I was close to him.

A few hours later, I get an even bigger surprise from my close, departed friend. Everyone is still in the den when Nora and I walk into Momma's bedroom to get something. We get the surprise of our lives when we see my dead friend's reflection in the mirror of Momma's dresser!

Drew looks sadly at me and appears to be trying to communicate, but it frightens me to see him as a ghostly image.

Nora and I scream and run out of the bedroom. I don't know what Drew is trying to tell me, because I don't stay in Momma's room long enough for him to utter a word.

I am glad Nora is with me so I am not alone during this experience. I am also glad that she is a witness to this event.

I wonder if Drew is going to stay and haunt our house. I hope not. Drew was my friend, but I want the dead to remain that way.

Drew may have unfinished business in his life that causes his spirit to not be at rest, and if so, he may think I can do something about it. There may be details about the circumstances surrounding his death that he wants to share with me.

Drew may be trying to reveal a secret. He could be trying to tell me that his death was not an accident. Was my friend murdered and is he trying to reveal who did it? I wonder if Drew's spirit is going to remain unsettled until truth is revealed or justice is served. I hope he is not relying on me to do it.

There is a reason why Drew revealed himself to me and allowed my family to witness the manifestations. Remembering that my mother was good friends with his, he may want to include her in helping to solve the mystery. His spirit seems to be trying to reach out to communicate with the living.

These two episodes leave me with a creepy memory of my dear friend—and an uneasy feeling as I wonder if he will appear to me again. I won't sleep well in Momma's bedroom tonight, but it is better than sleeping alone in my spooky room.

My awareness is heightened, and I am cautious when I look in the mirror. I try not to think about Drew or say his name, out of fear that this will summon his spirit. The mystery is never solved, and thoughts of the manifestations fade in time.

No one ever says anything negative to me about this experience, nor do they think less of me. It is just deemed as one of the many unusual events in our lives.

Sometimes it feels like something evil is lurking in my room, and it feels creepy in there. But I didn't sense an evil presence in the den when I experienced the bloody newspaper, nor in Momma's bedroom when I saw my friend Drew's face in the mirror.

The evil pervading my bedroom may be there because of the Ouija board that Linda left in the bottom of the cedar robe when she remarried and moved out of the house.

Me at 15.

A NIGHT TO FORGET

Sometime in 1973, our niece, Anna, goes with me to the theater to see *The Exorcist*. Both of us want to see the movie because it is scary, but we don't expect it to be as frightening as it turns out to be. I also want to see the movie because it is supposedly based on a true story, but this ends up causing me to be even more afraid.

No one else in our family wants to go with us. Even Momma declines the invitation, and she warns us not to see the movie.

It is the first time Anna and I go to the movies by ourselves, and it is night time, but we are determined to go see it. We are terrified by the end of the movie.

Momma comes to pick us up and sees the frightened expression on our faces. She was right—we shouldn't have exposed ourselves to the horror of the movie.

What you expose your mind to gets recorded, and it can be replayed over and over. Unfortunately, it can't be erased. The Spirit of Fear will use these types of experiences as tools to get people afraid. Then it will try to keep them fearful.

Momma says, "I told you not to watch that movie. I knew you would be afraid." Anna's mother tells her the same thing, and adds, "You are going to have nightmares." Both of them were right.

I am still shook up when we get home. While telling my family about the movie, Joe decides to have fun trying to scare me. He climbs onto the bar in the den and begins to mimic one of the scariest parts of the movie by pretending to turn his head around to the back of his head. I ask him to stop, but he continues doing it. Momma doesn't discipline him, so I give Joe a fair warning that I will hit him if he doesn't stop teasing me. He continues poking fun. I get mad and hit Joe so hard that he falls off of the bar. I feel awful for hitting him, but it seemed to be the only way to make him stop scaring me. I don't think he realized how afraid I had become.

I have never laid a hand on my brother, though he causes me pain constantly by playfully hitting, pinching and poking me, and by thumping my throat with his finger—so it took Joe by surprise when I wacked him. We both apologize later, and he doesn't pick on me again.

Spooked on
St. Michelle Avenue

Bedtime arrives, and I'm glad I don't have to sleep in my bedroom tonight. Daddy will not be home for a few more days.

I don't have nightmares about the movie, but Anna does. I soon put the frightening memories behind me, but Anna can't help thinking about what she saw in the movie. Over and over they are replayed in her mind.

I feel sorry for her when I find out that she is petrified and doesn't want to sleep in her bedroom. Sometimes she senses paranormal things in there, and seeing the movie has heightened her fears.

Anna sleeps at her other grandmother's house next door to them for six weeks after watching the scary movie. I am glad Anna's two brothers didn't pick on her and heighten her fears like Joe did to me.

STRANGE SOUNDS IN MY ROOM

Sometimes eerie thumping sounds similar to someone tapping their fingernail on a hard surface can be heard in the cedar robe in my room. It is accompanied by faint scraping noises as if something is dragging across the stack of games on the floor of the cedar robe.

I check to see if our small dog or some other animal is in the cedar robe, but no living thing has presented itself. The sounds are creepy, and it frightens me each time I hear them. I get used to the noises after a while, but I still don't like them.

One day my cousin Nora comes over for a visit. She never knows what to expect when she arrives at our house on St. Michelle Avenue, especially after the frightening experiences with my deceased friend Drew.

We hang out in my bedroom for a while. I am sitting on the bed and Nora is standing by the cedar robe as we casually talk.

Suddenly our conversation is interrupted by the thumping and scraping noises in the cedar robe. Nora has heard the strange sounds before, and she agrees with me that the noises are probably caused by an evil spirit that is associated with the Ouija board. I am tired of having to deal with it, and I want to get rid of the board. Nora and I decide to throw the Ouija board away.

We tell Momma what is happening as we walk through the den with the game, and we pray for protection as we walk to the garbage can by the road. I toss the Ouija board into the can, and Nora puts the lid on it. We are glad it is gone, and we relax as we eat lunch and hang out in the den for a while.

Then we decide to play a board game, and I head to the cedar robe to get it. While opening the door, I am startled to see that the Ouija board is back in the cedar robe!

I calm down when I reason that someone must have seen the board and brought it back into the house. Then I realize that they would have had to walk past us with the board. My fear returns.

Nora and I take another trip to the garbage can and pray all the way there. I toss the board in the can, and Nora places the top securely on it.

Then Nora sits on top of the can and playfully bounces on it to make sure the lid is secure. She grins and says, "Now the game can't get out." We laugh as we return to the house.

Nora and I stop in the den to tell Momma that we got rid of the game. Then we head to my room to get the board game that we were going to play earlier.

Nora looks on as I open the cedar robe. I coil back in fear when I see that the Ouija board is back in there again! There is no way this can happen, but it has. We run into the den and tell Momma about it. She is as shocked as we are by what is happening.

Nora and I devise a better plan to get rid of the Ouija board. We decide to burn it. I hope this will also rid the house of any evil spirits that may be attached to the board.

It is personal now between me and that board. We become brave in our attempt, because we know that God will protect us. Momma gets the matches while I pull the game out of the cedar robe.

As I carry it into the den, the planchette or plastic game piece begins to move around inside the box! This frightens me at first. Then I wonder if my movements are causing the pieces to move around.

I stop walking, but the planchette continues scooting around by itself inside the box!

The thumping and scraping noises become stronger, and I realize that they are the same sounds all of us have been hearing inside of the cedar robe for quite some time. It is the plastic piece dragging across the board, and the tapping sound is it banging against the inside edges of the box. All of us get scared this time, and Momma says, "Hurry up and get rid of that thing!"

Nora and I go out to the front steps and set the game on the top one. Momma stays in the house. I dump the matches out, and we begin to quickly light them.

Then something else unexpected happens. The box quickly burns, and the planchette melts, but the board won't burn! A strange blue flame dances around on the surface of the board, and blue smoke rises from it, but the board doesn't get singed or damaged in any way.

We try to burn it again and again, but the board will not burn. We get spooked and run into the house.

Momma throws the game away, and this time she ties the can shut. Nora and I sit on the steps and wait for the sanitation department to come by and get it. We are glad we don't have to wait long.

Then we return to my room and hesitantly look in the cedar robe to make sure the Ouija board isn't in there. We breathe a sigh of relief when we don't see it.

The next day, my bedroom has a different aura about it. There are no more thumping or scraping sounds in the cedar robe, and the room is warm. The atmosphere feels good, and it is peaceful in the house for a change.

A week or so later, my niece Tina wants to change bedrooms with me. Now that the evil presence is gone, I decide to let her have my room. It doesn't matter to me which room I am in, and I will be getting married soon.

After moving into the bedroom at the front of the house, I realize that I like it better than my old room. It is bright and cheerful, and no evil lurks in the closet.

A few weeks after this, tragedy befalls our family. I am out of town getting things ready for my wedding. Momma and Joe are spending the night at the camp. Jonnie and his family are the only ones at home when the house catches on fire!

*Spooked on
St. Michelle Avenue*

It happens in the middle of the night while everyone is asleep. Our next door neighbor saves their lives when he sees the flames and calls the fire department. Then he helps to get everyone safely out of the burning house.

My fiancé (whom I will call Charles because he wants to remain anonymous) and I are visiting a friend of his in the New Orleans area on the night of the fire. We are laughing and joking with the man and his family when I suddenly get the feeling that my family back home is in danger. Feeling the urge to pray for them, I excuse myself and step outside. I am out there for quite a while, interceding on their behalf. I want to go home, but Charles says it is late, and that he will bring me home in the morning as we had planned. I stay up most of the night praying.

My heart sinks with dread when we drive up to my house the next morning and discover that it has burned down! Linda is waiting there for us, to let us know that everyone got out of the house safely and to let us know where our family is. I thank her for coming and thank God for answering my prayers. He made sure my family got out of the burning house.

We are forced to move from St. Michelle Avenue. The house is beyond repair and is soon torn down. Only the front steps that Nora and I tried to burn the Ouija board on remain as evidence that a home once stood there.

The firemen said that a short in an electrical wire on a small appliance in the kitchen probably caused the fire, but I will always wonder if the Ouija board had anything to do with our home and all of our belongings being destroyed.

The timing of the fire was probably a coincidence, but I wonder if it was an act of revenge from the demon because we got rid of the game and evicted the evil spirit. Either way, neither of us have a place to call home.

My new bedroom is one of the rooms that have the most damage. My metal jewelry box and the costume jewelry inside it melted into a tight ball, and everything else on my dresser burned to a crisp, but my Bible that was lying next to the melted jewelry box did not burn or singe!

My cousin Nora and her family move back to Texas not long after this. A few years later, Nora marries Roger and begins a new life with him, but she never forgets the things that happened in our house on St. Michelle Avenue in the years between 1973 and 1975.

Jonnie Adair with his wife, Betty.
Their children are shown on the next page.

*Spooked on
St. Michelle Avenue*

Eliot & Jonnie Jr.

Kendra and Tina

As the years go by, our family never talks about the unusual things we experienced, but haunting memories surface once in a while, and I, too, think about the chilling encounters we had on St. Michelle Ave.

In 2011, I ask our niece Anna Labauve, then our cousin Nora Jewell, if they remember anything unusual that happened while we lived on St. Michelle Ave. Though neither of them kept in touch with one another over the years, both of them immediately mention the occurrence of the bloody newspaper, and Nora adds that she remembers seeing my dead friend Drew's face in the mirror.

The Ouija board comes into the conversation, and Anna recalls my bedroom as being the creepiest room in the house.

Years later, Nora wonders if the Indian heritage of our family is what causes some of us to have the ability to see and hear paranormal phenomena.

My cousin Nora and her husband, Roger Bayless.

Chapter 7

Family Lore

None of the people in our family who have experienced paranormal phenomena were interested in ghosts prior to our ghostly encounters. We were all taken by surprise when unexpectedly confronted with the strange events.

Nora told me that years ago they lived in a house that may have been haunted. Nora and her brother Curtis were young at that time.

The house they lived in was built in an unusual way by previous owners. A well was encased within a storage room. The rest of the house was built around the storage room, making the well the center of the house. I wonder if this was the owners' first attempt at indoor plumbing.

Swamped by Ghosts

The well may have been placed inside the house to keep it a secret, to have the water more accessible, or they may have had some other goal in mind. Whichever the case, it is unique. You could yell into the well and hear it echo down the hollow space.

Two doors led out from this unusual room. One door opened into the living room, and the other one opened directly into the kitchen.

Strange sounds which could be heard throughout the house were emitted from the well. The unusual sounds could be from a number of things.

The logical explanation would be that the well was picking up sounds that were in the house. Electrical appliances, running water in the pipes, and other daily activities may have been the cause. It might also have been the normal sounds a house makes as it settles and creaks.

As I dig for a deeper understanding and possible cause of the eerie sounds coming from the well, I can't help but wonder if the sounds originated from the ghost of a person who may have drowned in the well. This person's spirit may be stuck in the place where he or she died.

Another speculation is that the well may be a pathway to hell. The well may be picking up sounds from hell, since sound travels through water.

One can only guess at the cause of the eerie sounds, and I like to explore all of the possibilities.

Nora's family is watching television one day in the living room when all of a sudden they hear a loud noise like a gun shooting! They duck for cover.

Their parents cautiously look out of the front door, but they can't see well through the screened-in front porch. As far as they can tell, nothing is there.

Then another loud blast rings out, and the sound seems to be coming from the back of the house. They think someone is shooting at them, and they become frightened. Nora and Curtis huddle on the floor.

Uncle Wayne grabs his gun as he prepares to protect his family. They wonder who could possibly want to shoot at them. The loud noises continue, and they realize the sounds are coming from inside of the house—from the well room!

Cautiously, Uncle Wayne approaches the door leading to the well. Adrenaline is running high as he swings the door open. With gun in hand, Uncle Wayne scans the room for an intruder.

He doesn't see anyone there, but he becomes alarmed when he notices red liquid splattered all over the walls and floor. A few seconds later Uncle Wayne lowers his gun and exclaims, "Oh!" He realizes that the explosive sounds and red liquid are from tomatoes he recently canned in glass jars that had exploded. They laugh about it later, and it is still a running joke in the family.

Our Aunt Joyce had given Uncle Wayne (her brother) careful instructions on how to properly can the tomatoes. But something went awry, causing the jars to burst. Uncle Wayne never attempted to can tomatoes again after that.

THE AMITYVILLE HOUSE

Years later, Curtis becomes a soldier in the President's Air Force Honor Guard, and he is based at the Bowling Air Force Base in Washington, D.C. Curtis and two of his Air Force buddies get together one night and go watch the movie *The Amityville Horror*.

Right after seeing the movie, they are sitting down talking and drinking, when they decide to go spend the night in the basement of the Amityville house. It is a Thursday, somewhere in late 1979 or the early 1980s. Their intention to go there is to prove that all of it is a hoax.

When they get off of work the next day, they take off to upstate New York. When they get to the house on 112 Ocean Avenue, they see a fence around it and they also notice that the house is boarded up. There are "danger" signs and "no trespassing" signs on the property. Curtis and his friends aren't able to get near the house.

When Curtis tells me this story later, he makes a comment that he believes that if he and his buddies would have been able to enter the Amityville house that night, three drunk soldiers would have died in that house. There would have been three dead guys in that basement. Curtis believes that those walls may open up to the gates of hell.

DOUBLE OCCUPANCY

Curtis had been a skeptic of the paranormal until the year 2004, when he experienced things that terrified him and caused him to realize that he lived in a haunted apartment.

Curtis had moved into a one-bedroom apartment in Carrolton, Texas, and he was told that an old man lived in it before he did.

The old man moved into the apartment when the building was new. He lived there for many years—until he died. He was the only tenant the apartment ever had. Then the apartment was completely remodeled, and Curtis moved into it.

Curtis lives alone and is a very light sleeper. The least bit of noise wakes him up. Nothing unusual happens the first few nights Curtis lives in the apartment, but things begin to happen on the third night that hurl him into the world of the supernatural.

Curtis turns the lights off and climbs into bed. He dozes off to sleep, but he wakes up around 11:00 p.m. and notices that the kitchen light is on.

He gets up and checks the exterior doors to make sure no one has broken into the apartment. The doors are secure. Curtis turns the kitchen light off, assuming that he must have left it on. Then he goes back to bed, only to wake up a little while later to notice that the kitchen light is on again!

He goes back into the kitchen and looks at the light switch to see if there is a short in the wire, just like any other red-blooded American man would do. He reasons that there has to be a logical explanation for this to keep happening.

Then Curtis notices that the light switch is in the up position, like someone had turned it on. He becomes suspicious and wonders if someone is playing an elaborate trick on him.

Curtis looks in all of the closets, and he checks the doors to make sure they are locked. The apartment is secure, and he finds no one in his one-bedroom apartment. There is nowhere for anyone to hide in his small living quarters. He can't find any physical explanation for why this is happening. Perplexed, he goes back to bed.

Curtis is lying on his side in the bed. and he is not quite asleep yet, when he feels the mattress beneath him sink down as if someone is sitting on the bed next to him! Curtis is petrified to know that someone is in the bed with him. He cracks one eye open to look but doesn't see anyone. Curtis is not sure what to do. How does one get away from something he can't see? The presence is there for only a few seconds.

Curtis jumps out of bed and turns the bedroom light on, but he doesn't see anyone there. Then he realizes that the apartment is haunted. He wonders what he is going to do now that he knows there is a ghost in the apartment.

Curtis lies back down, but he soon notices that the light in the kitchen is on again. He goes into the kitchen, turns the light off, and goes back to bed. This goes on all night long. Curtis keeps turning the light back off, because he doesn't want a higher electric bill from the light being on all night.

He is unnerved by what is happening, but he is also getting frustrated. He wants the spirit to just leave him alone. Nothing else unusual happens for several days..

Then all of a sudden the same scenario occurs. Curtis turns the kitchen light off and goes to bed. Then he wakes up to see that the light is on again. This goes on all night...and begins to happen two or three nights in a row, at various intervals.

It seems like an amusement for the ghost—or a battle of wills between what Curtis wants and what the spirit wants. Curtis ponders whether he can send half of the electric bill to the ghost, since he is wasting so much electricity. Then he wonders if it could be something totally different. Perhaps the ghost is afraid of the dark.

A pattern begins to emerge. There will be periods of time where nothing happens. Then it starts back up again and will last one, two, or three nights in a row.

Sometimes when the light doesn't come on, Curtis is just as aggravated, because of the anticipation that it may come on. This becomes nerve-racking, and it begins to really affect Curtis. It is always the kitchen light that comes on. It is freaking Curtis out, and it is really spooky.

Curtis goes to the office to ask them where the old man was when he died. They say the man died in that apartment. (While telling me this story in 2011, Curtis said that he should have asked if the old man worked the night shift.)

One night, Curtis makes sure the kitchen light is out before going to bed. Then he wakes up and notices that the kitchen light is on again. He goes into the kitchen and turns the light off, but this time he lays down on the couch in the living room.

Curtis is spooked and can't go to sleep. He decides to try to get a glimpse of the ghost, to see if it is the old man. Curtis waits, and he expects the ghost to appear at any time. Suddenly the ghost does something unexpected. He turns the bedroom light on!

Curtis gets up and goes into the bedroom. He looks around and is not surprised when he doesn't see anyone in there. He turns the light out and lays back down on the couch in the living room.

A little while later the bedroom light comes back on again, and the specter's game continues. To Curtis, this game is not fun, and he is losing sleep over it. The ghost has eternity—he can do it forever.

The next day, Curtis goes to the office and tells them, "Something is going on in that complex. I don't know what it is, but I'm moving out." They offer him another apartment in that complex, but Curtis tells them, "No. That isn't going to happen." Curtis doesn't want to be anywhere around that spooky apartment. He's had enough of the shenanigans, of the ghost constantly turning the lights on and off, and of him repeatedly sitting on Curtis's bed.

Curtis Jewell

The old man may have been trying to scare Curtis out of the apartment. Later in the day, Curtis gets his stuff and leaves. He lets the ghost have the apartment.

THE SPIRIT OF MASION MADAME

Many years ago, our niece Anna Lebauve and her husband Coy moved into a haunted house with Anna's parents and younger brother. The rental was on Stadium Drive, near the school board and Terrebonne High School. All of them had moved back to Houma from another state.

The family suspects that a ghost is in the house when Anna begins seeing a female apparition who constantly follows her around the house while she is cleaning. Anna always sees the ghost out of her peripheral vision in her brother's bedroom, too.

The ghost has really dark hair and is evasive when noticed. No one in the house is afraid of the ghost. They accept the presence of the specter.

Anna's mother (our older sister) is skeptical about the paranormal. She always has been.

The apparition is not intimidating or a threat to anyone in the house, until one night when Anna and Coy are watching television in their bedroom. Coy is lying on the floor, and Anna is relaxing in the bed. Without notice, the ghost suddenly grabs both of them on the hip at the same time!

Anna and Coy both jump up and are puzzled by what is happening. Anna looks at Coy, thinking he grabbed her—and Coy looks at Anna, thinking she grabbed him. Then both of them realize that with the distance between them there was no way either of them could have touched the other. Both of them felt the spirit grab them at the exact same time.

It must have been a large being to be able to reach both of them at the same time, or it may have been more than one spirit.

A day or two later, Anna's mother is taking a shower when out of thin air a penny falls from above her. It hits her body and drops into the tub. She comes out of the bathroom trembling with fright as she tells everyone what happened.

Anna's mom had heard of the paranormal encounters we had over the years, but she never believed in that kind of stuff. Then she had a ghost in her own home but denied it to be factual until something paranormal happened to her. This experience made a believer out of her. Her doubts were dispelled, and Anna's mother believed there was a ghost in the house.

My niece, Anna Labauve.

Anna was frightened by what happened in their house, but she says that the scariest place she has ever been was our house on St. Michelle Avenue.

BEYOND THE GRAVE

Joe's daughter Natasha told me about ghostly encounters that she and her husband Mark had in a house they moved into in Raceland, Louisiana, around 2003. The house is close to the highway that takes you to New Orleans, and it is by the bayou.

A tragedy hit Mark's family in 2007 when Mark's twin brother Matthew drowned in the bayou. It happened about a mile down the road from where Mark and Natasha live.

Not long after the accident, Mark and Natasha are startled when their radio in the living room suddenly turns on by itself! It is blaring full blast. After this, every once in a while the radio unexpectedly comes on. There is nothing physically wrong with the radio.

Another unusual thing starts happening around this same time. Mark and Natasha will be doing something in the living room and suddenly hear one of the bedroom doors slam!

They believe it is probably the ghost of Matthew doing these things. Mark and Natasha aren't afraid of the ghost of his brother. It is like a prank Matthew is playing on them when the radio turns on by itself. It always blares full blast and comes on when they least expect it.

Over a period of time, the paranormal activity ceases.

Twins usually have a close bond between them. They are connected emotionally and mentally. If it was Matthew, he sought out his twin brother and did things to cause his presence to be known.

Ghosts usually manifest by turning the water, lights, television set, or other things off or on. They also choose to make themselves known by flushing a toilet, moving things around, and sometimes by speaking to humans.

They make noises by slamming doors, stomping up or down stairs, and banging or knocking on walls, doors, or windows. There are many other ghostly manifestations people have witnessed.

Mark and Natasha Kraemer.
Mark is wearing his Cajun Nikes (white shrimp boots).

Mark's sister is involved in a Houma Ghost Hunt Society. She is the occult specialist of that group and can tell if activity in the ghost hunts is paranormal.

In 2011, I found out that two of our nephews are ghost hunters. Both of them became interested in the subject after hearing our ghost stories over the years, as well as from having ghost encounters of their own. They began looking for opportunities to witness more of the strange events.

Our niece Anna says, "Most of our family members try to stay away from ghosts that are haunting them, while others in our family go out looking for them."

SKELETONS IN THE BASEMENT

One day a real estate agent suspected that a certain house in Bayou Black, a town outside Houma, was haunted. This agent told one of our ghost hunter nephews and his two friends about it. The three of them went out there to check it out.

When they go in a certain area of the house, our nephew becomes nauseated and starts vomiting. It has been said that sometimes the presence of a spirit can produce a noxious smell or cause humans to vomit.

The three guys know something is not right, and they go down into the basement to investigate further. They don't see the ghosts that are manifesting, but they do find a chilling piece of evidence that something is amiss. They come across the femur bone (large leg bone) of a human! Then they find more human bones.

They don't know where the bones came from, and they realize they need to call the police. The police come and investigate the age of the bones. They discover that the bones are very old and are from an Indian burial ground on the property.

People who cut the grass and did other yard work would find the bones and throw them into the basement. That is why the bones were there.

I have heard that sometimes the spirit of a person will haunt the area where their body was improperly buried or where their grave has been desecrated.

Chapter 8

Gouauxst Avenue

Linda and Carroll Bourgeois

Linda and Carroll were married in June 1974. A few months later, they bought a house on Gouaux (pronounced "goes") Avenue in the suburb of Houma. They also became owners of a smaller house at the end of their long driveway. Linda and Carroll moved into the large house and rented out the smaller one.

Previous owners had also rented out the small house. Unfortunately, one man who had rented the house was said to have committed suicide by slitting his throat on the back steps! Upon further investigation, the police deemed the death a murder. The man's throat was cut deep, and it was cut from the opposite direction than the man would have been able to do. The weapon used was held with the opposite hand that the man used. The family of the deceased man continued living in the rental.

A year later, on the anniversary of the man's death, his sister committed suicide on those same steps.

A boy who lived in the rental after Carroll and Linda owned it killed his stepfather on the same back steps that the man and his sister died on!

It is strange that three people who lived in the back house died on the back steps of it. When the rental became vacant again, Carroll and Linda decided not to rent it out anymore and they turned off the electricity.

Their two children, James and Elisha, began using the back house as a place to hang out in. The parents put a ping pong table in the back room.

Once in a while when we are visiting, my daughter Shannon hangs out back there with the children. Except for Carroll and Linda, we are all unaware that three people have died on the steps leading out of the back room.

Late one evening, I am in the back house with the children. James and I are playing ping pong, and the girls are just hanging out. Suddenly an eerie presence begins to pervade the room.

I begin to get the feeling that someone is watching us. I can tell the children feel it, too, because they look nervous.

Then someone states that they are ready to leave. I tell them, "Let's all leave. It's getting late." We bravely head out the back door and break into a gait once we get into the dark yard.

Shannon and her cousin Elisha enjoy each other's company and sit on the back steps of the small house often. They are still unaware of the tragic events that took place there. It is a convenient place for them to relax after playing or walking on the balancing beam in the back yard.

I am not yet aware of the deaths that occurred on the steps, either. I am sitting on the back steps of the small house with the girls one day, when I suddenly sense that someone is watching us. It is the same feeling I had when we were in the back room of the house.

I look around as I wonder if it is a neighbor. I don't see anyone, but I know that someone is there. I try to ignore it, but I can't shake the uneasy feeling.

Goose bumps begin to rise up on my arms and at the nape of my neck, and I realize that it is a spirit. Then I sense that it is right by us! The girls are laughing and talking, but they suddenly become quiet as they nervously look around. I know that they probably sense the eerie presence, too.

Without saying a word, all three of us descend the steps and quickly leave the area. I tell Linda about our experience, and she reveals the history of the rental. This explains why we experience such strange things at that back house.

Some ghostly spirits seem to not be at rest, and they can remain where the person dies due to an unnatural or untimely death. Thus, a haunting occurs. In this instance, two murders and a suicide had occurred in the exact location. What are the odds of that happening? Slim to none, unless there is something that links the events together.

Demonic spirits may have influenced the people to commit these tragedies. Demons such as the Spirit of Death try to persuade people to kill others or themselves.

The complete history of the house is not known. Perhaps other previous renters or owners of this house have died in it or on the back steps.

It was around this time that Carroll and Linda generously opened up their home to me and my two children for several months.

We hastily place our belongings in the back house for storage, and we settle down to eat supper in Linda and Carroll's kitchen. After supper we talk and joke around. It's getting late, and it is dark outside.

My baby son Stephen starts crying. He has been suffering from an earache. I look for his medicine and realize it is in the back house. I know which box it is in and that it won't take long to get it, but I don't want to go in there alone.

Haunting memories of the three tragic deaths that occurred at the back house, and of the eerie presence the children and I felt while back there, flash in my mind. I am glad when Linda offers to go with me into the dark, spooky house.

I hold my flashlight tight as we enter the front door. Fear tries to grip me, but thoughts of my crying son make me determined to continue on our quest to get the medicine.

The house looks a lot different at night than it does during daylight hours. I begin to feel uneasy as we walk through the living room and sense that someone is intensely watching us. It is unnerving, but it doesn't stop me from continuing on to the room where the medicine is.

Linda stands near me as I take the medicine bottle out of the box, and she is in front of me as we walk back through the living room. All of a sudden we hear a loud moan right by us! It scares us half to death, and we take off running back to her house. I may have died of fright if Linda had not been there with me.

I wonder if it is the ghost of one of the three people who died in that house years before, or if it is our mother coming back from the dead. It sounds similar to Momma's voice, and she used to moan like that to playfully scare us when she was alive.

(I never went back into that house again at night. I don't think Linda and her family ever did either.)

Carroll and Linda experienced many paranormal phenomena throughout the forty years they have lived on this land. At least four spirits have been seen in their house. Two of the entities appear often and have never bothered them. They usually appear and do things when there are changes in the house.

These two spirits, a man and a little girl, get active when Linda and Carroll's son James and his family stay with them for periods of time. The spirits manifest when the family moves into the house, and they manifest again when they move out.

The man ghost is aware of Carroll's family, and he seems curious about things that go on in the house. Carroll and Linda are not afraid of him. The man looks like he is in his sixties, and he wears a white t-shirt and khaki pants. Linda thinks it is the first man who had died in the rental before they purchased the property.

The ghost is inquisitive, and he watches Carroll while he does things in the house. Carroll is a carpenter by trade and often purchases new tools or gadgets. He is also an avid fisherman, and once in a while he buys new supplies for his large tackle box.

When Carroll buys something new, the man ghost comes to check it out. Sometimes Linda walks in and sees the male ghost standing by the new tool. He is looking down at it as if he is wondering what it is. Carroll is so involved in what he is doing that he doesn't notice the ghost standing beside him.

After Linda and Carroll have lived in the house for twenty years, Linda sees the ghost of a female child of about seven or eight years old. The girl walks from the hallway by Carroll and Linda's bedroom and into the kitchen. The girl has blonde hair and wears colonial-style clothing. Her dress has puffy sleeves and flairs out from the waist. Linda can see through the girl. The man ghost is more solid than she is.

The girl doesn't frighten Linda, and she wonders if the girl is the one who is the prankster in the house. Often items around the house are missing and are later found in a place they had searched already.

On one of these days, Carroll can't find his pocket knife. Both he and Linda search everywhere for it, and they still can't find it. Carroll walks back into their bedroom, and the pocket knife is lying in the middle of the bed! It was not there before. They had searched the room well.

One day Linda can't find her driver's license or debit card. She searches all over the house for them, but they are nowhere in sight. Finally she is forced to go get another license. She pays for the new one and returns home. Upon entering the house, she sees the two cards lying on the floor in front of the couch! Linda knows the cards were not there before she left the house.

NOW THEY SEE HIM—NOW THEY DON'T

Carroll and Linda are not at home one day when they get a call from a neighbor informing them that the police are at their home. They are responding to a complaint from the neighbor, who saw an intruder in Carroll and Linda's house.

Soon neighbors gather to see what is happening. The neighbors and police officers see the shadow of a man in the house, going from room to room and turning the lights on. The police officers freak out. All of them have their guns drawn and the house surrounded when Carroll and Linda get home.

Using their key to get in, they search the house and the attic thoroughly, but they find no one there. There are no signs of a forced entry, and the man could not have left the house unnoticed. The officers and neighbors are positive that they saw the man.

Then Linda realizes that it may be a spirit in the house. They discover that whatever or whoever was in the house had taken a can of tomato juice from the cabinet, opened it, made a large circle on the floor, and then placed the empty can in the center of the circle.

Carroll says that the tomato juice is probably a substitute for blood. The red circle on the floor is probably part of a satanic ritual. Carroll and Linda hope they got home before the ritual could be completed. I shudder to think what may have happened if they hadn't.

The situation is a mystery, and it may never be solved. One of the officers tells Carroll and Linda, "Man, I don't know how y'all live in this house, because I know what I saw."

After the police and neighbors leave, a family member and his wife start laughing and playfully say, "Let's have a séance." They don't really intend on doing it, but upon hearing these words, Linda and her friend run out of the house. They don't want anything to do with it. Linda doesn't want to open a spiritual door to evil spirits.

After everyone leaves, the house is eerily quiet. Linda watches television until the station goes off the air at two o'clock in the morning. Then she tries to do something else to help herself not think about what had happened and to not wonder if the intruder might return. She finally calms down and goes to sleep.

A TERRIFYING SPIRIT

Another spirit Linda sees in their home is that of an old woman who looks like she is in her nineties. She wears a long white dress that seems to flow as if wind is blowing it. The dress has long sleeves that gather at the wrists and do not flow like the dress does. The collar goes all the way up to her neck, and a little ruffle is at the edge of it.

Linda has a terrifying experience with this spirit after going to bed one night.

Carroll is fast asleep. Linda is lying on her back and saying her prayers before going to sleep.

All of a sudden Linda sees the spirit of the old woman hovering over her! The spirit is not solid. A shadowy mist surrounds her and follows her as she moves. The mist moves as she moves. The man and the girl ghosts have normally been seen to walk across the floor, but the old lady floats. The woman looks mean, and her face is full of hate toward Linda.

Without warning, the spirit begins choking Linda! She is terrified and tries to pray aloud, but she can't speak because of her constricted throat. Linda prays in her mind for God to help her.

She keeps hitting Carroll on the arm to wake him up, but he won't budge. It seems to take forever to get the evil spirit off of her. Linda is so afraid that she sticks like glue to Carroll for the rest of the night. She is so close to him that they look as if they have merged into one person.

Linda believes this spirit is a demon. I agree, and wonder if the spirit had anything to do with the three deaths in the rental behind their house. I also wonder if anyone died in this part of Linda and Carroll's house before they moved into it. This area of their home has an eerie atmosphere about it.

Carroll and Linda became born-again Christians, and Linda doesn't tell fortunes with the Bible anymore. They started going to church, and they now live a Christian life.

One day they decided to remodel their home. Carroll is a carpenter, and he did the job himself. After tearing down their back bedroom, some of the paranormal activity taking place in that area of the house stopped.

BACK FROM THE DEAD

Momma died of heart failure in March 1985. Not long after this, Linda purchased an interesting book on how to contact the dead. She missed Momma very much and was eager to try to contact her in the spirit world.

Linda reads only halfway through the book when she decides to give it a try. After Carroll goes to sleep, she starts calling for Momma in whispered tones. She waits for a response, but she gives up a short while later when nothing happens.

Suddenly Linda is startled when something thumps her on the back of her head! She thinks, *What did I do? What did I conjure into our bedroom?*

Linda wants to scream and her heart beats wildly, but she doesn't want to wake Carroll up. She wishes she would have finished reading that book to find out how to get rid of the spirit.

The rhythmic thumps on her head continue, and she becomes afraid that it is Momma coming back from the dead. Momma was a prankster, and she used to do these kinds of things to us when she was alive.

Linda wanted to contact Momma in the spirit world, but she didn't know in what way Momma would manifest to her. Linda thinks it probably wasn't a good idea to try and conjure Momma from the grave, and she wonders how to get the thumping to stop.

Finally, Linda becomes brave enough to knock the hand away from her head. This action sends Carroll into a panic, as he suddenly wakes up and wonders who hit his hand! It was Carroll who had accidently tapped Linda on the back of her head while he was dreaming.

This experience scares Linda so bad that she never tries to contact Momma again. Not long after this, Momma begins visiting Linda, but in a different way than she imagined.

During the first year of Momma's death, Linda has surprise visits from Momma through dreams. Linda enjoys the long conversations they have. Some may say that these are just dreams Linda is having, but Linda and I believe that it is the spirit of our departed mother coming to visit her, like Linda desires. It is possible that departed souls can somehow enter dreams.

Momma coming back in this manner may be less frightening than if her ghostly spirit would suddenly appear beside Linda, especially after Linda's scary ordeal when she thought Momma had come back from the grave. Just the thought of a seeing a dead person is frightening, even if it is a close family member or friend—but a dream is less invasive.

Linda wonders if the girl ghost in their house is the ghost of our departed mother, because each time Linda sees Momma in her dreams, Momma becomes younger and younger. The last time Linda sees Momma in one of her dreams, Momma is four years old and can't talk to her.

Time is irrelevant in eternity. Spirits of the departed aren't stuck in their mortal body, so they should be able to appear to humans in dreams—and from different stages of their life.

Eternal souls seem to be the age of their death while appearing in a ghostly form on earth.

I had the same kind of dreams about Momma during the first year of her death, and it seemed more like visitations than dreams. The only difference between my dreams and Linda's was that Momma was an adult in my dreams, and she looked like she did the last time I saw her alive. Neither Linda nor I knew the other one was experiencing these visits from Momma until we talked about it years later.

Momma talks to me in a way that seems real and current. She asks how we are doing and carries on a long conversation. The communication seems more like something Momma would say or ask me if she were alive, rather than just talking to a ghost. It is more personal than abstract, like a dream would be.

The first time I had one of these dreams was right after Momma died. She began the conversation with a question, and she looked puzzled as she asked me where her clothes were.

Momma's question bothered me. I felt guilty because I had taken some of her clothes after she died. I was glad she continued talking before I had to awkwardly answer her question.

I gave this some thought upon waking up and realized that this must have been a visitation from Momma, because I hadn't felt guilty at all for bringing some of Momma's clothes home with me. I knew that Momma probably wouldn't mind. The rest of her clothes had been donated to a thrift shop to be used by others. Thinking about it now, Momma may have just been curious about where the clothes went.

We siblings had gotten together at Mom's house after her funeral, and each one of us chose something of hers to keep. One of my sisters picked Mom's jewelry. Another wanted the beautiful crocheted blanket Momma had made, but I chose to keep some of her clothes. They would have gone to the thrift store along with Momma's other belongings if I hadn't taken them. I also liked that the clothes had the smell of my mother still lingering on them. Having some of her personal things was like having a part of her with me, and it helped me to deal with the grief of losing her.

Momma's wardrobe was important to her when she was alive, and it was a special thing between Momma and me. We were the same size and had the same taste in clothes. Sometimes she would let me wear her clothes when I spent a few days with her. Going through Momma's closet with her had resulted in some of my fondest memories.

After this dream, I wondered if Momma knew I had taken some of her clothes. I felt bad about it until I remembered that Momma wasn't angry or scolding me in the dream for taking her clothes. She just seemed genuinely interested in knowing where the clothes were. Maybe it helped to bring a closure to her death.

Momma could have actually come back from the dead and searched for her missing clothes when she didn't find them in her house. But her asking me about the clothes in my dream causes me to wonder if she knew I had taken some of them. Why would she want her clothes now, and how would I return them to her?

According to reports of paranormal phenomena, sometimes when a person is attached to certain personal items or their money when they were alive, their spirit continues that behavior after their death. Some of these spirits are not at rest, and they wander around in search of these missing items. I hope I didn't do anything that would cause my mother to not rest in peace.

Swamped by Ghosts

Toward the end of my dreams of Momma, she says that she has to go. It is as if she has come from somewhere and now has to return there. Later, Linda comments that Momma says she has to go at the end of her dreams, too.

A few days after Daddy died, I had a vivid dream of visiting him in heaven. I believe this was an actual experience—and an answer to my prayers.

I am missing Daddy, and I'm upset that I didn't get a chance to tell him goodbye when he unexpectedly departed this world. Also, our relationship was a strained one, and I pray earnestly that somehow I will know that Daddy loved me.

After going to sleep on this night, I dream that I am transported to heaven. I know where I am and find myself walking through a beautiful field of grass. It is a peaceful and serene atmosphere.

Ahead of me is a body of water, and a man is standing by it. I immediately know it is Daddy. As I walk closer, he slowly turns around and smiles at me. It seems as if he is expecting me.

Then Daddy casually walks toward me. He looks happy, and he seems much younger than when I saw him last. Now he looks like he is in his early thirties.

When Daddy gets near me, his smile widens and he opens his arms in anticipation of a huge hug. With a firm embrace, my Daddy lets me know that he loves me.

Then he takes a step back and says, "Hey, baby girl." That is one of his nicknames for me. I ask, "How are you?" He replies, "Good. I live right over there," and points to his left.

I am about to look over there, but I get a distinct feeling that I am not supposed to—that I am here only to see Daddy. He smiles again and says, "I've got to go now, but I will see you soon." I feel complete—and loved. At this moment, the dream ends.

Over the years, I have had two dreams of Daddy visiting me. Both of them were a direct response to events that were happening around me. My stepmother Betty was with him in one of those dreams. They both helped by giving me advice.

My daughter Shannon has the same type of dreams that Linda has had, and she doesn't know about Linda's encounters.

Shortly after a woman that was close to Shannon died, she came to Shannon in dreams. The woman became younger and younger in each dream Shannon had of her during the first year of her death, and then Shannon saw her as an adult once a year for a few years.

The woman was concerned about Shannon and her children right before she died. In Shannon's dreams, the woman always asks how the children are doing. She shows genuine interest in their welfare, like she did when she was alive.

Sometimes God speaks to us through dreams or visions in order to warn us. Other times He uses dreams to direct us in making important decisions when we ask for His guidance.

This has happened to me many times. One of those times was when we were on our way home from town. My husband was driving, and our two young children were riding in the back seat of the car. God stopped us from getting in an automobile accident.

I saw a large truck coming from the opposite direction and recognized it from a dream I had days before. The truck hit a bump and swerved in the direction we would have been if I hadn't warned my husband to pull over.

On two different occasions, I was applying for a job, and I asked God to show me if it was where I should be. Both times I got a clear answer through dreams. In my first dream, I dreamed of the school that I would be working at, just days before I actually started working there. I hadn't seen the school before my dream. In my second dream, I dreamed of a student that I would be working with, and smiled to myself upon meeting her a week later.

God works in mysterious ways. It is possible that He allows angels and departed souls to enter people's dreams to help comfort those who are bereaved or to guide them.

The subconscious mind is always active, even during sleep. What causes the contents of most dreams remains a mystery. This is also a time of opportunity for evil spirits to influence us or interject wrong thoughts into our subconscious mind.

When we are awake, what we allow into our mind will affect us. We need to guard our thoughts and dwell on godly things. Our conscience mind filters our thoughts, but our mind is limited in the process of selection, to reject or accept thoughts while we sleep. Demons will use this opportunity to influence us.

Fatigue, intoxication, illness, wrongful desires, and negative thoughts are the most susceptible times of invasion of our subconscious minds.

DADDY & BETTY'S GHOST

In 1975, soon after I get married, Dad and Mom divorce. Momma often complains about Daddy to her friend and co-worker, Betty Daigle. After Betty tells Momma that she can change him, Momma introduces Betty to him. Momma watches to see if Betty can change Daddy.

Daddy likes Betty and starts going to church with her. He becomes a Christian, and soon Daddy and Betty get married.

Everyone is happy. Daddy dotes on his new wife and is out of Momma's hair, and Betty has a husband whom she dearly loves.

Daddy in 1993.

Years later, Daddy and Betty move to Texas, but they don't stay there long. It may be because they miss being in Houma, or maybe because they have witnessed strange things happening in their new home.

Betty and Lee Adair.

Carroll and Linda go visit them, and paranormal phenomena begins to happen the night they arrive.

When they wake up on the first morning there, Carroll notices that the underwear he wore when he went to bed is gone! It disappeared from his body while he slept. Linda denies any part in this.

They search the room well but cannot find it. The missing underwear is never found.

Carroll wonders how his underwear got off of him without waking him up. It must have been a ghost who did it, and he or she had to be pretty good to steal Carroll's underwear without waking him up. The ghost may have gained the skill by doing this to other people who previously owned the house.

I wonder how the family would have reacted if they would have seen Carroll's underwear floating down the hall as though the ghost was wearing it.

Right after they get into bed the next night, Carroll and Linda become aware that the covers are slowly being pulled off of them! They are annoyed but are used to this sort of thing happening at their house. They hope the spirit will just go away, and they don't respond to the invisible prankster. They pull the covers back over them and go to sleep.

Later in the night, the unseen specter slowly pulls the covers off of them again. It wakes Linda up, but she just ignores the spectacle as she pulls the covers back over them and goes back to sleep.

When Carroll and Linda wake up the next morning, they wonder where the covers are. They figure that they must have kicked them off of the bed during the night. They expect to find the covers in a heap on the floor next to the bed, but instead they discover that the covers are neatly folded at the foot of the bed!

I wonder if this has happened to others who lived in that house or stayed in that bedroom. Maybe the ghost doesn't like strangers in what it deems to be its home, and possibly its room.

It is possible that a person died in that bedroom, and now he or she is haunting it. Having a ghost in there could also be the reason why the house was up for sale when Daddy and Betty purchased it.

Not long after these incidents, Daddy and Betty move back to Houma. They don't mention if they had any ghostly encounters in the house, nor do they say whether the house being haunted was one of the reasons they moved out of it.

SCREAMS IN THE NIGHT

Carroll often works overnight hours during the first years of their marriage. On one such night in 2003 or 2004, Linda goes with her daughter and son-in-law to see *The Blair Witch Project*. It is a scary movie about a female college student, and it was said to be a true documentary.

Thinking the movie is based on a true story causes Linda to be afraid, and Linda believes the scariest part of the movie is when the three college students run through the woods screaming.

Linda returns home and is alone in the house when she goes online and does research on the movie to find out more about it. Then she turns off the computer and goes to bed.

Linda is startled awake at two o'clock in the morning by the sound of blood-curling screams! As she jumps out of bed, she recognizes them to be the voices of the three college students from the movie, and she realizes the sounds are coming from the office next to her bedroom.

Upon entering the office, Linda sees the computer on—and that the part of the movie where the students run through the woods screaming is playing over and over again on it. Linda is puzzled as to how the computer came on, because she knows she turned it off.

She turns the computer off and returns to bed. A few minutes later she jumps—and thinks, *What the heck*—when she hears screaming in the office again. Linda wonders if there is something wrong with the computer as she turns it back off.

Linda turns around to leave the room, when the computer comes back on again. This scenario happens several times. By this time Linda is shaking with fear. Her nerves are completely unsettled as she unplugs the computer and quickly closes the office door on her way out of the room.

Linda knows why this particular part of the movie is playing over and over. It is because that part of the movie scared her the most. Her fears are met with the opportunity for an evil spirit to use it against her. It seems as if the demon will not be denied the chance to inflict horror upon my sister.

Linda settles back into bed. Seconds later she is horrified when she hears screaming coming from the unplugged computer! She doesn't get out of the bed this time. Linda knows there is nothing she can do to stop the frightening sounds.

The screaming on the computer continues, but Linda tries not to pay attention to the frightening disturbance. After a while the screaming stops.

She knows the computer is unplugged and that this should not be happening. She refuses to go back into that room that night and face the spirit that is using her computer. Linda prays for God to protect her, and she finally drifts off to sleep.

She is glad when Carroll returns home the next day. Together they try to come up with a logical explanation for what happened, but they cannot find one. They know it is a demonic manifestation taking place.

Linda didn't expect a demon to harass her after watching that scary movie, and now Linda is stuck with those haunting memories and images. The part of the movie that Linda was most frightened of is the part that came back to haunt her through her computer.

Demonic spirits could be attached to movies like this, and viewing them may invite evil spirits into anyone's home.

A CLOUD OF LIGHTS

Once in a while Carroll sees another spirit that he believes to be a demon because he feels evil emit from it and is afraid. It is not in a body form. The evil spirit is like a cloud of a thousand small white lights. The only way Carroll can get this spirit to leave is to rebuke it.

Linda is sound asleep one night when something shakes her awake. She opens her eyes and is horrified to see this same spirit by their bed!

It is the demon in the form of a cloud, and it has what looks like a thousand small lights inside of it. Linda prays for what seems like hours, but it is actually only about ten minutes. The demon finally leaves.

In 2009, Carroll and Linda came to visit us in Arkansas and stayed for about four days. Not long after they returned home, I witnessed the same cloud of many lights in our trailer that they had encountered in their home.

I got ready for bed and was in our master bathroom, when the evil spirit suddenly appeared about four feet in front of me! I would have been petrified if my husband had not been nearby. He was on our bed, which was about ten feet away.

I had to walk right past the strange-looking cloud of many small spheres of light to get out of the bathroom and away from the spirit. I sensed evil but didn't feel threatened by it. I got the impression that the spirit was here looking for Carroll and Linda. It disappeared a few seconds after I left the bathroom, and I never saw it again.

Also in 2009, Carroll and Linda's neighbor and their married daughter Elisha happened to come to visit them at the same time. All of them were standing in the doorway talking, when their daughter and neighbor suddenly saw something black quickly fly from the kitchen and into the closet next to the living room! They told Carroll and Linda about it.

SOMETHING LIGHT FOR SUPPER

In March 2010, Carroll and Linda come to visit us in Arkansas again. They both return to work the day after they get back home. On the way home from work, Linda stops at a local eatery to get something to bring home for supper.

Linda is alone, and she puts the food on the kitchen counter as soon as she comes into the house. Then the phone rings. Linda goes into the living room to answer it. I am the one who is calling her. She tells me that she is really hungry and will eat while we talk. When she returns to the kitchen to retrieve the food, it is not on the counter where she left it! The food has disappeared.

Linda carries the cordless phone with her as she looks all over the kitchen for the missing food. I hear doors open and close as she looks in the refrigerator, the stove, and the microwave. Linda even looks in the washer and dryer.

She looks in all of the same places again, and she searches for the food in other parts of the house, though she has not gone in there. I detect exasperation in Linda's voice when she can't find it.

Linda is tired of these pranks and is frustrated as she says with great force to the ghostly prankster who probably took it, "I want my food, and I want it now!" A few seconds later she looks in the stove, and the food is in there! It is as if the ghost was thinking, *Uh oh, I made Linda mad. I'd better return her food.* Linda can't help but wonder if it is the ghost of our mother playing a trick on her.

In August 2010, Linda and Carroll settle down to an evening of relaxation as they sit in their living room watching television. It is quiet in the house when unexpectedly both of them hear a thunderous boom as if something ran into the wall in the kitchen.

Moments later they hear another crashing sound in the closet near the living room. The spirit seems to be trying to get Carroll and Linda's attention. It couldn't be trying to hide, since it was making enough noise to attract attention.

They know it isn't their inside dog or cat making the noises. The small dog is lying on the couch by Linda, and the cat is lying on Carroll's lap in the recliner.

Carroll and Linda acknowledge what is happening, but they are not overly alarmed because they view it as just another unusual thing they have experienced. I wonder if it is the same spirit that their daughter Elisha and a neighbor saw the year before.

These are just a few of the many paranormal things that have happened in Carroll and Linda's home in the past forty years they have lived there.

FOUR MEN AND A BABY GHOST

Carroll and Linda's house isn't the only one in their neighborhood that is haunted. They know of at least one other haunted house near them.

Years ago, four bachelor Christian men from their church rented a house a few streets over.

The men frequently heard a baby crying in the house, but there was not a baby anywhere near their home. The crying baby kept them up at night.

None of the four men were married, yet they were still being kept awake by an unseen child. They wished there was a way to comfort the baby or get it to stop crying so they could get some rest.

This ghost story puts a new twist in the phrase, "Children should be seen and not heard." They could have made a new sitcom series and called it *Four Men and a Baby Ghost*. This experience may have discouraged the men about having children altogether—or maybe it gave them a taste of fatherhood!

Chapter 9

A Ghost Town

I married my fiancé Charles in March 1975, eight months after Linda married Carroll. Charles is Cajun and is Carroll's first cousin, who is also a Cajun. My wedding took place two weeks after our house on St. Michelle Avenue burned down.

Plans had been made for us to get married in the house on St. Michelle Avenue, like Linda and Carroll did, but the house was gone and I didn't mind our wedding being in my older sister's home instead. She and her husband had been gracious and took us in when our house became unlivable after the fire.

Charles was born and raised in New Orleans, and he had lived in the upper ninth ward before we got married. He rented a double complex on Community Street, in the little town of Arabi,

Louisiana, for us to live in after our wedding. This part of the area is called "Old Arabi," because it is where the first settlements in this area were.

Arabi is located in St. Bernard Parish, between the Lower Ninth Ward of New Orleans and Chalmette, Louisiana. It is within the Greater New Orleans Metropolitan area.

Arabi is a suburb of New Orleans and is right over the Orleans Parish line. It was a part of New Orleans at one time, and is only about ten miles from the famous French Quarter.

Arabi sits along the east bank of the Mississippi River. Though the town wasn't established until the nineteenth century, there is a lot of history in this area of St. Bernard Parish.

St. Bernard was once part of Orleans Parish—until a law was passed in the 1880s stating that slaughterhouses could not be located within the city limits of New Orleans. For this reason, local politicians convinced those in New Orleans to let St. Bernard Parish separate from the Orleans Parish government.

Arabi began as a community known as "Stockyard Landing" because of the many stockyards and slaughterhouses here. It was also called "cow town" because of the many cows that were raised and sold in this area.

Years ago there was an ice house at the end of Community Street. Trains would depart from it after stocking up on ice blocks and with meat from the slaughter houses nearby.

New Orleans and Arabi were originally settled on the natural levees of high ground along the Mississippi River. Living near the water made trading and traveling easier for the new residents.

Swamped by Ghosts

Over time, Old Arabi was dubbed a "ghost town" because of the many businesses that closed down. I call it a "ghost town" for a different reason. After living here for a while, I realized there are spirits of the departed troubling this area. Many of the houses around here are haunted. I wonder if most of the paranormal phenomena are because of the town's turbulent past.

Much of the population in those days consisted of the most wild and undesirable characters, which included galley slaves, trappers, gold seekers, pirates, and city scoundrels.

By 1800, more than fifty percent of the population was African-American. New Orleans had played a major part in the Atlantic slave trade. It had the largest slave market in the South. Two-thirds of more than one million slaves brought to the South had arrived by the forced migration of the slave trade. This could be one of the reasons why New Orleans is considered to be one of the most haunted places in America.

The southern music known as the blues has deep roots in American history. The blues originated on the southern plantations in the Mississippi Delta just upriver from New Orleans in the nineteenth century, when African slaves and their descendants sang as they toiled hard in the cotton and vegetable fields of their masters.

This music began as a mixture of spiritual hymns, work songs, field hollers, and drum music which came from that sad time of their life. Most often it was an expression of their loss of hope, the desire of returning to their native land, or the dream of what could be.

The blues music of today can be very joyful or it can be sorrowful. It comes from a deep feeling of the heart. It doesn't have to be sad, but often is about the loss of love and other trials of life.

A Ghost Town

Slave dressed in sack cloth, bound in shackles and chains.

In the War of 1812, the British tried to conquer New Orleans, but forces led by Andrew Jackson prevailed, with the loss of two thousand British soldiers. The battle was fought in Chalmette on January 8, 1815. It is known as the Battle of New Orleans, and the site is located a few miles down the river from where we lived in Arabi.

By 1840, New Orleans had become the wealthiest city in the nation. Tens of millions of dollars were made during the Antebellum Period, and New Orleans was a prime beneficiary.

New Orleans was a major port during the Antebellum era. Its port exported and imported huge quantities of goods to be traded up the Mississippi River. The river passes through New Orleans and St. Bernard, and was filled with steamboats, flatboats, and sailing ships.

Electricity was introduced to the city of New Orleans in 1886, and there was a limited use of electric lights in a few areas of town a few years before this.

In the 1890s, most of the city's public transportation system relied upon mule-drawn streetcars on most routes, and a few steam locomotives were used on the longer routes. Eventually they used electric streetcars. Some are still in use today and can be seen on St. Charles Avenue.

Some of the ships and river boats docked at the port in Old Arabi.

Forty years after Hurricane Betsy, Hurricane Katrina brought havoc to New Orleans on September 29, 2005, causing many hardships for the people in the city and the surrounding areas. Many homes, businesses, and lives were lost during this time. But hard work and persistence is making New Orleans strong again.

THE LEBEAU MANSION

In 1851, Francois Barthelemy LeBeau purchased property in Old Arabi and began building the Greek Revival style house that is now called the LeBeau mansion. It was completed in 1854.

A few months later, Francois LeBeau died. He never got to enjoy the elegant home he built. The 10,000 square foot, two-story plantation had sixteen rooms, one interior stairway, an attic, and an octagon-shaped cupola (tower) on top of it.

The LeBeau mansion was once the largest plantation south of New Orleans, and up until 2013 it was one of the oldest buildings in St. Bernard Parish.

It sat along the bank of the Mississippi River, next to the Domino Sugar Refinery at the end of LeBeau Street. Over the

A Ghost Town

years the house served as a hotel, a brick factory, and an illegal casino.

The plantation remained in the LeBeau family until the Friscoville Realty bought it in 1905 and began developing Friscoville Avenue into a gambling area for locals and those in New Orleans.

In 1907, Friscoville Avenue in Arabi hosted at least five gambling halls. All of them were located along the 100 block of Friscoville Avenue. They were right outside of the Orleans Parish line, and were easy to get to from New Orleans by the Canal Street Car Line.

The LeBeau mansion was operated as the "Friscoville Hotel" for the next twenty years. It was a hotel and gambling house into the mid-twentieth century.

*The LeBeau mansion in 1912,
when it served as the Friscoville Hotel.
This photo was taken by George François Mugnier.*

The New Orleans Fronton was built in 1925 for gambling.

All of these establishments operated until 1952, when they were shut down because of a statewide ban on illegal gambling.

In 1928, the Jai Alai Realty Company bought the LeBeau plantation, and for the next ten years it was used as an illegal casino and as the "Cardone Hotel," which was a boarding house for casino dealers. Gun turrets were built into the closets.

From 1938 to 1967, the beautiful mansion was sold to various owners. It was during this time that an abusive man, his wife, and their newborn baby lived in the house.

In 1967, the local land baron Joseph Meraux bought the LeBeau mansion, and it was vacant for many years. It slowly deteriorated.

In 1986, the pre-Civil War house was vandalized, and even the medallions were taken from the fireplace. The vandals set fire to the house, and the fire destroyed a lot of the interior and most of the roof. From that point on, the house was uninhabited.

Workers tried to restore the old house three different times, but each time they did work on it the second story floor would cave in. After the third time this happened, they gave up trying, and the restoration of the LeBeau mansion was never finished.

In 2003, the structure was strengthened and plans were in place to renovate, but it was boarded up after Hurricane Katrina devastated St. Bernard parish in 2005.

On Thursday, November 21, 2013, the LeBeau mansion burned to the ground, and an important and beloved landmark of the New Orleans area was lost. Seven suspects were arrested who had been in the house that day under the influence of alcohol and marijuana. According to a WDSU TV News report (New

Orleans, November 25, 2013, 5:40 pm), deputies said that the suspects told them they'd been looking for ghosts.

GHOSTS IN THE LEBEAU MANSION

Some people say that the LeBeau plantation was haunted. Most of the old houses in the neighborhood near the river are. From 1989 to 1993, my husband and I rented one such house. It was not far from the LeBeau mansion. We experienced ghostly manifestations almost every day in the four years we lived there.

One day while living there our eleven year old daughter, Shannon, has a friend over visiting. Shannon takes a ride with me later that day to bring her friend home. We casually talk about the LeBeau mansion as we pass it, and we tell Shannon's friend that our landlord owns it.

The three of us decide to get a better look at the house. I park the car, and we cautiously walk into the huge yard of the magnificent mansion.

I am excited to get a closer look at the LeBeau plantation, and am pleasantly surprised to get the chance to speak with the groundskeeper who lives in a trailer next to the house.

The nice man offers to give us a tour of the large house, and we carefully walk around in the vacant structure. The house is falling apart, and we can't go upstairs because of damage from the previous fire. But I am still in awe at the size and beauty of the place, and I can imagine how it must have looked when it was first built.

Swamped by Ghosts

We don't get to see the inside of the cupola (the top section or tower), because the weakened wooden stairwell outside is too dangerous to climb.

I would have loved to have seen the entire house before the fire of 1986 destroyed so much of it, but I was grateful to get a look at it that day. I am disappointed that I didn't bring a camera. I didn't know we would be going inside of the mansion, and didn't want to bother the nice man by coming back again. Later I regretted not returning. The man probably wouldn't have minded.

Around this time Shannon and I got a chance to speak with an elderly woman who lived in a huge house on Friscoville Avenue, which was near the LeBeau mansion. She shared a story that her mother had told her many years ago—one of the stories that explains what may have happened in the LeBeau mansion that caused it to be haunted.

With sadness in her voice, the woman said, "An abusive man, his wife, and their newborn baby lived in the LeBeau mansion many years ago. They had a fight, and the woman went into the tower above the house with her baby. It was in the winter and was very cold up there. The baby died from the cold."

I had heard some of the ghost stories about the LeBeau mansion over the years. People brave enough to get close to the scary house late at night said they heard a baby crying.

Several times over the years, nearby residents reported seeing a mysterious light in the vacant mansion's cupola glow in the moonlight hours. A few people I know have told me they

A Ghost Town

have seen the light in the cupola come on, even though there was no electricity in the house.

One girl lived by the LeBeau mansion. She and her brother would sneak onto the property and climb the outer stairs all the way to the cupola at the top of the structure. They put sticks in the windows to hold them up. Then, they ran back down the stairs and to the street. They would turn around and see that all the windows were closed! It was scary for them, but it was also fun.

Other unusual phenomena have occurred in the LeBeau mansion. One story is of a man who went into the house often as a child. His great-grandmother worked as a caretaker there. Every time they went into the house they heard footsteps on the two floors above them. They would go up there and check it out and wouldn't see anyone there. They would also hear screams, moans, and the sound of bottles breaking. The man heard that a lot of people had died in the house, and he heard that slaves were buried in the large opening under the house.

This man lives in the same block as the LeBeau mansion. His house is also haunted, and it sits on the very spot of the slave shacks where the slaves resided. Many graveyards were established all around the edges of the property. He sees strange things outside at night. People dressed like they were from a different time area have been seen walking down the street. This man got so used to the unusual phenomena that he sees it as just another thing to talk about.

The man knows of other stories of the strange phenomena that took place in the mansion. One story took place in the 1970s. The LeBeau plantation was being rented out to a family whose girl was forcibly thrown from a window of the cupola, but it wasn't by a human.

Stories have circulated about the history of the LeBeau plantation. One legend has it that the LeBeau family mistreated the slaves that worked for them. Some of the slaves died as a result of severe punishment. They were buried around the perimeter of the plantation grounds. The spirits of the deceased slaves made their way back to the house and began haunting the LeBeau family. One family member after the other was driven to insanity. Two members of the LeBeau family hung themselves on the second floor of the mansion.

SLEEPLESS NIGHTS

Most people stay away from the spooky-looking house, but I know someone who lived in it for a while. I will call him Gerald. I am one of only a few who knows of the unusual things that happened while he was there.

Like most of the residents in the area, Gerald had heard the ghost stories over the years. But Gerald was a skeptic. He would have to see something paranormal to believe it. Moving into the mansion gave him that chance.

Gerald was relaxed and smiled as he told me about moving into the beautiful mansion years ago, but appeared nervous as he began telling me about unusual things he experienced while living there. He thought he lived alone in the large house, but soon realized that resident ghosts lived there, too.

He wasn't living in the house long when strange things began to happen.

A Ghost Town

One night Gerald gets comfortable after sliding under the covers of his bed. All of a sudden he hears a baby crying!

He is perplexed and searches the house to see if anyone has broken in looking for shelter. Not a soul is there—not a live one, anyway.

Gerald climbs back into bed and tries to ignore the pitiful cries, but they continue. He can't go to sleep because of the crying, but doesn't know what to do about it.

After a while the cries gradually subside, and the house is quiet again. Gerald drifts off to sleep.

When morning comes, he searches the house again for a possible break-in, but doesn't find anything out of place.

As days go by, Gerald occasionally hears the pitiful cries of this baby, and he begins to believe in the possibility of the supernatural. But what happens next makes a believer out of him. This tough, grown man admits to being scared.

Gerald pulls the covers up to his neck after climbing into bed, like he usually does. Just as he gets comfortable, he hears a baby crying again. Gerald tries to ignore it and hopes the disturbing noise won't last long. Then something else unexpected happens, and it sends chills down his spine.

Gerald's covers slowly begin to be pulled off of him! He looks up to see the faint outline of a woman at the foot of the bed, and he just knows it is a ghost. Gerald's fear is intensified by knowing that he is alone in the house with the spirit, but he calms down a little when he remembers that God is only a prayer away.

An unusual chill has been invading the room since the spirit appeared. Gerald's covers are at the foot of the bed, and

Swamped by Ghosts

he wants them back. They are all that separates him from the ghost, and Gerald wants to hide under them. For now, they are his security blanket.

Using all of the courage he can muster, Gerald quickly grabs the covers and pulls them tightly over his head. He contorts his body into a fetal position, and he holds onto the covers with his legs and hands so that he won't lose them again. He knows that he is outmatched for a blanket tug-of-war. Also, Gerald doesn't want to see any more of this specter that is interrupting his sleep and peace of mind.

The covers are still over Gerald's head when another unexpected thing happens. He hears a woman sobbing in the corner of the bedroom!

The crying is heart-wrenching, and Gerald calms down as he listens to the pitiful sounds. He knows this is the voice of the female ghost who took his covers a few minutes earlier.

Gerald remains still for a while to see what the ghost may do next. The crying gradually subsides, and warmth returns to the room. Gerald soon drifts into a restful sleep.

The next morning Gerald realizes that he can't stay in the house any longer because of the things he has witnessed, and he begins looking for another place to live.

Gerald later told me that he saw and heard other strange things in the LeBeau mansion, but had gotten nervous and didn't want to talk about it.

Maybe the ghost wanted Gerald's warm blanket to wrap around herself. But in view of the stories I have heard and what

Gerald has witnessed, the female ghost seemed to want the blanket to bundle her crying infant, to protect the suffering child against the bitter cold temperature of that fateful night of its death.

The ghost may have waited just long enough for Gerald to warm the blanket with his body heat before trying to take it from him, and she became upset when he took the blanket back.

It seems that the spirits of the frantic woman and her newborn baby were unsettled spirits who remained stuck in the century-old house as they relived that fateful day the baby died in the house.

The wailing probably came from a distressed infant that cried until its death many years ago, accompanied by the mother's sorrowful cries as she helplessly watched the baby die in her arms. Unspeakable grief remained within those walls.

The LeBeau mansion in more recent times.
Photograph © Corey Balazowich, used with permission.

ANOTHER MANSION NEARBY

There is another elegant mansion near the site of the LeBeau plantation. This large house is probably not as well known as the LeBeau mansion, because it is hidden by a wooden fence that surrounds it, and it is not near the road. This mansion looks like it may have been a hotel and gambling house at one time, because of the palm trees and a built-in swimming pool in the large yard.

One of the walls of the mansion has a gaping hole that was probably blasted out of it by a cannon ball from the War of 1812. The hole was gilded over with gold. This must have been done as a showcase of the artillery damage to the building.

Cannon balls and other artifacts that are found in people's yards and along the riverbanks in this area of town also come from the Chalmette Battlefield, which is not far from here.

The mansion is old and has a history of its own. If only it could talk, I wonder what mysteries would be revealed and what secrets remain buried within its walls. Since the old deserted mansion is in a ghost town, I wonder if it also has resident ghosts within it.

A SPIRIT ATTACKS ME

Soon after we get married, Charles gets me a kitten. She grows up fast. One day the cat does something unexpected. I am sitting on the chair in the living room. The cat is lying on my lap purring as I pet her. Suddenly the cat stands up in my lap, arches her back, and hisses at something in front of us that I don't see. I have never seen her do this before.

Her claws are out, and she begins to slash at the unseen entity. Then the cat growls and lunges in the air as if attacking something or someone. Then she lets out a loud cry and runs into the kitchen.

I am scared and become even more frightened when I sense a strong evil presence in the room. Goose bumps appear on my arms and neck. I begin to frantically pray for God to protect me. The evil spirit finally leaves about ten minutes later.

The next day I am lying on my back in the bed after Charles leaves for work. The cat is outside. Suddenly I get the feeling that someone is watching me from the open bedroom closet, and I sense that it is an evil spirit.

Dread washes over me, and knowing that I am the target of a possible appending attack frightens me. I feel like something is focusing on me, like a cat will do before attacking its prey. I don't know what to do, so I remain still and pray for God to protect me.

I don't see the evil spirit, but I am aware that it is slowly coming out of the dark closet. Memories of the frightening experience I had about three years ago when an evil spirit choked me fills my mind. Terror strikes a familiar chord inside of me. My heart beats wildly as I lay helpless against the invisible entity approaching me.

I sense the impending spirit picking up speed as it nears the bed. I feel like prey and expect the spirit to attack me at any moment. I feel defenseless, and I wonder if it will try to take my life.

Suddenly the evil spirit jumps on top of me! I am petrified and lay totally paralyzed beneath it. It feels as if my whole body is weighed down by a strange force. I wonder if this is the same spirit who jumped on top of me and choked me three years ago.

The feeling is different than if a human held me down. The spirit is very strong, and I feel powerless against its strength. It is dominating me like a lion on top of its prey. I sense intense hatred toward me, and I can tell the evil spirit wants to harm me.

I am alone in the house while having to deal with this evil spirit. I can't fight the demon with my own strength, because I can't even move. The spirit has me pinned down on the bed.

It is a supernatural being and possesses supernatural strength. It has an advantage over me in this way, but I serve a God who is much stronger than any demon.

I try to call on Jesus to come free me, but no sound comes out of my mouth. My throat is also paralyzed. I say a frantic prayer in my mind and know God answers me when the spirit suddenly jumps off of me a few minutes later.

I am still visibly shaken when I get my Bible and sit at the kitchen table to read it. I gradually calm down and say a prayer of thanks to God for coming to rescue me.

I know why the evil spirit attacked me today. I brought this upon myself. Though I am a believer in Christ, I recently allowed a sin into my life.

The demon knows this and is taking advantage of the situation. My sin opened the spiritual door that allowed this demon to come into our home and into my life. I ask God to forgive me and to make me in right standing with him again.

God used this situation as a warning for me to repent of my sin. He used it as a teaching tool, rather than for the destruction of my body and soul. God used this opportunity to guide me back into his protecting grace. I was given another chance—a rude awakening.

Christians aren't perfect. We mess up sometimes. But Jesus is never far away. He hears our cry for help, and He comes to our rescue. He never leaves us. We walk away from Him.

When we repent, God takes us back with open arms (Psalm 143). He is a gracious God, and He loves us more than we realize.

God also warns us not to do it again. One sin leads to another one, and then another, until we are enslaved again to the lusts of the world.

God desires for us to be holy and set apart for him. He gives us the Bible as a guide to help us achieve that higher calling.

Chapter 10

No Safe Place

We live in this house for three years. Then Charles and I move down the road to Chalmette, Louisiana. Our daughter, Shannon, is born a few years later. Nothing paranormal happens in the three years we live here—that we are aware of.

Then we move further down the road to another rural town. It is also in St. Bernard Parish.

We only notice one unusual thing in the house. Some of our things get put in a different place in the house, and at times the missing items are never found. This kind of paranormal phenomena is referred to as typical poltergeist activity.

We attend a church that is in our neighborhood. A new church building is later erected on the land to accommodate the growing congregation.

I begin discerning that something is not quite right during some of the services in the new church, and whatever it is interferes with the movement of the Holy Spirit.

We soon discover that satanic rituals are taking place in the nearby wooded area of this block of the subdivision. I wonder if that is causing the unsettling disturbances in the church.

Occasionally, Shannon and others in the congregation see a black, human-shaped shadow in the baptistery area downstairs. I teach Children's Church in the room behind it.

Shannon and a few others also see a human-shaped shadow in the open area upstairs. It is near the room where my husband sits to work the sound system during the services.

I don't see the spirit, but I know when it is around. I get an uneasy feeling, and I sense that someone is watching me. Sometimes goose bumps appear on my arms, and the hairs on the back of my neck stand up.

A few years go by. It is 1983, and I am eight months pregnant with our son Stephen. Shannon is three years old. We hear loud, urgent knocking on our front door. A female is yelling, "Help!"

I open the door, and a pitiful-looking woman stands before me. The stranger is wet, and she has green slimy grass in her hair and all over her body.

Swamped by Ghosts

A pungent swamp smell hits my nostrils. I am wondering if the woman got in an automobile accident and ended up in the stagnant water of the canal that lies just beyond our short street.

The woman looks scared and tired. I feel sorry for her as I open the door and let her into our home. She goes straight to my rocking chair and flops down in it.

The woman begins acting strange as she tells us what happened, but I reason that she may be in shock from the ordeal she has been through.

The woman tells us that her baby died. She looks sad as she holds an eight-by-ten framed photo of a girl close to her chest. Sympathy fills my heart as I glance at Shannon, who is on the other side of the room, and I think about my unborn child.

As the story unfolds, we realize that the woman is mentally unstable. While the woman is looking at me, Charles eases into the kitchen and calls the police to report a possible accident and the woman's mental condition.

I casually move closer to Shannon, feeling the need to protect her. The woman gets quiet and stares ahead as if she is in her own little world. While she is distracted, I take Shannon by the hand and casually walk with her to the open area of the kitchen. This way we are near Charles and a safe distance from the woman.

The movement catches the woman's attention. Then she notices Shannon, and a strange expression comes over her face. I sense that something is wrong, and I pick Shannon up.

The woman slowly stands up and gently places the photo in the chair. Then she casually walks toward us. I am not sure what to do and I feel responsible for what may happen, since I am the one who let her into our home.

The woman says, "What a pretty girl. May I hold her?" I want to scream "No!" and run away from the woman's outstretched hands. But I think it best not to get the woman upset or make any sudden movements, so I casually take a few steps backwards and pretend not to hear her.

Charles is about to hang up the phone. I take comfort in knowing that he is nearby and that the police are on their way.

The woman looks puzzled as she gets closer to us and stares at Shannon. Then she yells, "That is my daughter!" Charles hears what the woman is saying and quickly walks over to us.

Then without warning, the wild-looking woman lunges toward us and tries to grab Shannon! Panic sets in and weakens me for a moment. Then adrenaline surges through my body and sets me in motion.

I devise a plan and take control of the situation. Quickly handing Shannon to Charles, I whisper, "Go in our bedroom and lock the door." The woman calms down once Shannon is out of sight. I am able to redirect the woman and persuade her to leave our home.

But she doesn't go far. The woman plops down on our front lawn. I am relieved that at least she is out of our house. Soon the police arrive and pick her up. I vow to myself that I will never open our door to strangers again.

The policeman calls us back later in the day to tell us that the woman lives on the street behind us. He also confirms to us that the woman does have mental problems. She has been in and out of a mental institution.

The police officer informs us that the woman does not have children. The photo belongs to her sister. She took the photo from her sister's house and jumped into the canal behind our subdivision.

I wonder if the woman tried to take her sister's child and was locked out of their house.

We are relieved to think this woman is out of our lives.

*Here, I am 8 months pregnant with Stephen.
Shannon is 3 years old.*

Some people who are deemed mentally unstable are actually demon-possessed or influenced by evil forces. One-third of Jesus' ministry was in delivering demon-possessed people. They were set free, and their minds were restored.

Evil is usually attracted to innocence. Evil tries to harm the good. This lady zeroed in on my daughter. I hope she finds peace within herself and gets delivered from her torments.

In 1985, Shannon is five years old and Stephen is two, when we encounter the mentally unstable woman again. The children and I are casually looking around while waiting for a prescription to be filled at the local drug store.

Shannon and Stephen are looking at coloring books while I glance at something on the other side of the isle from them.

Suddenly Stephen giggles and takes off running down the isle—as little boys do. I tell him to come back as I run after him. Shannon and I stop dead in our tracks when we see that the same woman who tried to kidnap Shannon from our house a few years ago has suddenly appeared at the end of the isle.

She says to Stephen, "Come here, little boy," as she leans over and stretches out her arms to grab him. Stephen doesn't notice her as he continues running full blast in that direction.

With an evil-looking grin on her face, the woman says in a scratchy, witch-like voice, "I've got you now…," as she slowly advances toward Stephen. I follow quickly behind him. She looks like a sumo wrestler by the way she walks with her legs out and arms extended.

Stephen immediately stops when he sees the wild-eyed woman. My heart races wildly as I continue advancing the few more steps to my son. It seems to take forever to reach him.

Shannon is frozen with fear because she remembers the woman whom she thought was a witch because of the slimy grass all over her.

I grab Stephen, and we don't look back as we quickly run away from the woman. I am relieved when we return to the safety of our home, and I hope the woman doesn't remember where we live. But this isn't our last encounter with this mentally unstable woman.

Stephen, two years old.

A few months later, my children and I see the same wild-looking woman in the lobby at the movie theater. I am glad she doesn't see us. We duck into the ladies' restroom to hide from her, and I hope she doesn't decide to come in here.

We sneak back down the hall about ten minutes later, and Shannon peeks around the corner to see if the woman is still there. The fear on Shannon's face informs me that we are still in danger, and I motion for her to come with us as we head back to the restroom.

Feeling trapped, we are forced to wait until the woman walks into the movie we were going to see. Then we quickly exit the theater. Relief washes over me to know that we are safe and that we were able to avoid a confrontation with the woman.

I don't let bad situations keep me down. I remain positive as I enjoy life and my children. I don't want us to live in fear, but I am more cautious now. I watch my children like a hawk.

Shannon is eight years old and Stephen is five in 1988 when we move from our home in Violet and rent a duplex in Chalmette. It is in the center of town and close to the park. We put everything that has happened behind us and begin anew.

I am glad to be away from the neighborhood where the mentally unstable woman lives, but I am aware that she comes into town. We live close to the movie theater where we last saw the woman.

Stephen & Shannon in front of the duplex

Sometimes I sense an eerie presence in this house, but it doesn't last long. It is during this time that items in the house are mysteriously placed in other rooms or become missing. We look all over for them, but the items are never found.

A SPIRIT IN OUR CAR

One day Shannon is sick and stays home from school. She rides with me to get Stephen from school at the end of the day. I park the car in front of the building to wait for the school bell to ring. We are both deep in thought as we sit quietly in the front seat.

Suddenly both of us hear a deep moan right outside my open window! We look at each other in bewilderment. Then Shannon says, "What was that?" I shrug my shoulders as I tell her, "I don't know." I am glad Shannon heard it, too. It seems like someone is trying to scare us.

I look around and don't see anyone. Then I glance down to see if someone is stooping down by the car. No one is there. I glance in the rear view mirror for the culprit, but not a soul is in sight. Not a living one, that is.

The moan sounds creepy, and is just like the moan Linda and I heard in her back house years ago. Fear grips me as I wonder if it is that same spirit. If so, it has come all the way here looking for us or it has been here all along. I was hoping to never encounter that spirit again.

I don't want to get out of the car to go get Stephen, because whatever caused the sound is out there. I feel safer in the automobile, though the windows are rolled down.

A few minutes later, Shannon and I hear it again! This time the eerie moan is closer and louder because it is coming from the back seat of our car!

Whatever is doing this is in the car with us. It has to be a spirit because the back door of the car didn't open for a human to enter it, and the back windows are closed.

Shannon and I quickly exchange glances, and our eyes are wide with fear. I have the urge to flee but can't, because I have a child in the car with me and another child that will soon arrive.

Without a prompt, Shannon joins me as we begin praying aloud for God to protect us. With each of the challenges we encounter, we learn more and learn how to depend on God to get us through them.

Then the school bell rings, and children come pouring out of the building. I am reluctant to leave Shannon in the car alone with what seems to be an invisible threat, but she doesn't want to come with me.

A few seconds later, Stephen exits the front of the building, and I am glad I only have to walk about twenty feet to reach him.

Usually Stephen jumps into the back seat of the car, but this time I insist that he ride in the front seat with us. Stephen asks me why, and I reply, "You don't want to know." I am relieved that he seems satisfied with my answer and doesn't inquire further into the subject. I don't want him to be afraid.

I look around the car and under it before getting into it, to make sure I didn't accidently hit someone when I pulled in. No one is there—that I can see, anyway.

On the way home, Shannon and I continue praying to ourselves. We occasionally exchange glances as we wonder if we are bringing the spirit home with us or leaving it behind.

I am relieved when we don't hear the moaning sounds on our ride home. Our prayers worked. We never hear this strange moan again.

If this wasn't the spirit of our departed mother, it may have been a demon, a "familiar spirit" as described in books I've read about spiritual warfare.

A familiar spirit is a demon who stays around a person for a long period of time and gets to know him or her well. The familiar spirit can imitate that person while the person is alive as well as after death. Some demons trouble families from one generation to the next.

OUR KIDS ARE IN DANGER

I am relieved that we don't hear the strange moaning again, and that we haven't seen the mentally unstable woman while living here, but something happens that is just as frightening.

Three young men try to kidnap our two children and their two friends while they play in our neighbor's yard!

A week later, an older man of a different nationality is brazen as he attempts to kidnap one of the girls as she yells for help while banging on our front door! Shannon and I spring into action and make sure the man doesn't succeed.

Shannon runs down the stairs two at a time to open the door for the girl, while I distract the man by yelling through the open window, "Call the police and get the gun!" It is the only thing I can think of to say that would deter the man long enough for Shannon to get down the stairs.

The man is about to grab the girl when he hears me yell and stops to look up at me. He hesitates just long enough for Shannon to open the front door and pull the girl into the safety of our home. Then she quickly closes and locks it. It was a close call.

It is around this time that we watch the movie, *I Know My First Name is Steven*. It is a true story about a boy who was kidnapped from a department store while shopping with his family.

The story is similar to what happened to our children, and of our plight at the drug store. The boy even had the same first name as our son.

Right when we think we are in a safe place, new dangers arise. Now we realize there is no safe place. Knowing that the men may return, we decide to move from this rental and away from these predators.

The National Center for Missing & Exploited Children:
1-800-843-5678

Chapter 11

Haunted House of the Rising Sun

Friends just happen to be moving out of a beautiful mansion in the New Orleans area that we fell in love with on our first visit there a few years ago. They ask if we want to rent the house. We realize this is a great opportunity and decide that we want to live there. Excitement builds up in us as we make plans to move into the mansion.

We move into the elegant mansion in November 1988. I am thirty years old, Shannon is eight, and Stephen is five.

The house is huge. Fireplaces grace six of the large rooms. None of them are in working order, but they add style to the rooms and reveal a bit of history about the hundred-year-old house.

The dining room is the center of the house. It has five doors leading from it. Just as all roads led into and out of Rome during the days of the Roman Empire, in this house all doors lead to the dining room.

The mansion was built in the 1890s and cozily sits on the bank of the Mississippi River. The house has a peaceful and inviting atmosphere about it, but it is also one of the most frightening places I ever lived.

What starts out as a dream come true becomes more like a nightmare as we witness ghostly manifestations almost every day of the four years we live here.

My previous experiences with the paranormal seem mild compared to what takes place in this haunted house. Some of the ghostly phenomena are included in this chapter, but all of them are told in detail in my book, *Haunted House of the Rising Sun*.

Stephen & Shannon on the front porch of the mansion.

We move into the mansion hoping to have peace and security, but instead find active spirits in the house and on the land it sits on. Other homes in the neighborhood are also haunted.

Three ghosts regularly make themselves known to us in the house, at least one ghost resides in the smaller house in the back yard, and another ghost is occasionally seen in the loft of the carriage house.

This is an old town, and things that happened back in the 1800s or earlier could be the reason why there is so much ghostly activity in the house and the surrounding area today.

It is also possible that the mansion is haunted because of the three old graves that are discovered in the back yard after we move out of it. The graves are marked by a makeshift construction of old bricks.

The back yard.

The cruelty to the slaves many years ago may have also caused some of the hauntings in the mansion.

It could truly be a ghost town due to the barbarous slave trade that was common practice at that time, because of the debauchery of the surrounding area, or both reasons.

It seems as if the ghosts are waiting for our arrival, and unusual things begin to happen just hours after moving into the mansion.

Night arrives. Beds are put together and furniture is in place, but unopened boxes are everywhere. I am still organizing boxes and unpacking the items we will need tonight. As I am walking past the front door to bring a box up the stairs, three loud knocks suddenly startle me. We are not expecting visitors, and only a few people know that we have moved. It is more like banging on the door than knocking, and it sounds urgent. I put the box down and quickly answer the door.

No one is there, and an automobile is not parked outside. Bewildered, I look around and wonder if someone is playing a practical joke on us. Then, I realize what is happening—as a bone-chilling presence brushes past me as I slowly close the door!

I don't see the spirit, but major goose bumps appear on my arms and the nape of my neck. Dread washes over me, and I am thinking, *Oh no, I have just let a spirit into our home!*

I lock the door, but it doesn't make me feel safe from the evil presence. A spiritual battle begins, and so does the onslaught of paranormal activity. I pray for God to protect us, and I have faith that He will.

Past experiences have sensitized me to the presence of spirits—be they ghosts or demons. I have also become more aware of spirit manifestations that occur around me.

It is after eleven p.m. when we settle into bed. A few minutes later, we hear what sounds like heavy chains rattling loudly and dragging across the floor of the attic! My heart beats faster as I listen to the strange noises. The children hear them, too, and come into our bedroom to tell us.

All of us look toward the ceiling and speak to each other in whispered tones as we wonder what is causing the sounds. I try to think of a logical explanation and conclude that it is probably rats in the attic, but I change my mind when I realize that even the huge river rats that are in this area couldn't make such a ruckus or drag those heavy chains around.

Then I begin to wonder if a person is in the attic. With this thought comes a frightful childhood memory of the horrible experience my family and I had when an escaped murderer hid in the attic of our home for two weeks. It also reminds me of when Linda and I saw the figure of a man in our attic when she was nine years old and I was seven.

Usually I wouldn't think such things, but past experiences have made me cautious, and my mind is open to such possibilities. Now I know that anything is possible, no matter how strange it seems. Ironically, my daughter is now the same age as I was when the escaped murderer hid in our attic.

Another scary thought is that the Jackson Barracks Prison is not far from here. They have had prisoners escape from there.

There is also the possibility that foreign sailors may have jumped ship at the nearby river, and that they are looking for a place to hide from the authorities. That has happened before in this area of town.

The thought that ghosts may be in our attic also enters my mind, but I dispel the thought out of fear of what else may happen if the house is haunted.

The clanging noises do seem to indicate that this old house is haunted. It may be the same eerie presence that brushed past me at the front door a few hours ago. This is just as frightening as the possibility of a stranger hiding in our attic.

A few minutes later my racing heart slows down, as I push these memories aside and realize the strange noises have stopped. We quietly wait to see if the eerie sounds return. The house remains quiet.

Shannon and Stephen return to their bedroom, only to come back into our room a short time later when all of us hear noises coming from downstairs!

It sounds like the tinkling of the dirty dishes that were left in the kitchen sink. I washed the supper dishes, but later left a few dishes in the sink to be washed in the morning.

We calm down when we realize it is probably just a rat in the sink moving the dishes around. I am not afraid of rats, so I volunteer to go take care of it. Shannon offers to go with me.

As we walk down the back staircase, we hear water running full blast in the kitchen and the tinkling of dishes moving around in the sink. We aren't as brave now, because we know that a rat can't turn the water on.

Shannon and I look at each other with confidence and lock arms as we continue toward the kitchen, knowing that we can run back up the stairs if we need to.

All of a sudden we hear a new noise. It is the familiar sound of creaking followed by dull thumps, as though the doors on the kitchen cabinets are opening and closing.

A moment later the noises stop. I am hoping that any intruder has gone out of the back door of the kitchen. I motion for Shannon to stay where she is as I continue on to the kitchen door. She gladly complies.

Glancing into the kitchen, I see that the small room is empty. I also notice that the back door is locked. This is puzzling, because whoever was in the kitchen would have had to pass by us on the way out of the room.

I look in the sink and expect to see a rat or other small animal in it, but instead I see that the dirty dishes that were in it are gone! The dishes have vanished!

Shannon and I look around the kitchen for the dishes, but they are nowhere in sight. I open the kitchen cabinets to see if by chance the dishes are in there. I discover that the dishes are not only washed, but are dried and neatly put on the shelves in the cabinets!

We try to find humor in the situation. Shannon laughs and says, "You should leave the dishes dirty in the sink every day, and maybe they will be washed for you!"

I tell her, "Whoever washed the dishes must like us—and may be welcoming us to our new home." We laugh as we turn to leave the kitchen.

"I am relieved to know that an intruder is not in the house, but feel just as threatened when suddenly I get the strange feeling that something unusual and evil is in the room with us! Shannon looks at me, and I can tell by the frightened look on her face that she feels it, too. We quickly leave the room and run up the stairs.

We tell Charles and Stephen the unusual story, and they are as surprised as we were when we saw it. We don't tell them about the evil presence.

All of us are tired as we settle back into our beds on this unusual first night in the mansion. The house is quiet as we turn the lights out.

All of a sudden we hear loud footsteps like someone very large and wearing heavy boots is stomping up the front staircase!

Shannon and Stephen run into our bedroom through the door that connects our bedroom to theirs. The loud footsteps go past their bedroom and stop at our bedroom door.

I still want to believe there are logical explanations for the unusual things that are happening in the mansion. I reason that someone must be playing tricks on us.

I expect to hear laughter in the hall, when without warning resonant pounding on the bedroom door sends all of us into a panic! It is so forceful that we see the heavy wooden door shake.

There are three loud knocks, and then the house becomes quiet again. It sounds the same as the three loud knocks we heard on our front door earlier tonight.

We expect the door to swing open, but the house remains quiet. The silence has us on edge as much as the loud banging on the door had caused us to be. We don't know what will happen next or where the intruder may be.

We don't know what is on the other side of that door. I ask myself if we should hide or run—if we should fight or flee. Adrenalin races through my body, and danger seems imminent.

None of us are the type to be easily scared, but most people would react the way we are if they were in this situation.

Whoever it is seems angry and is not here to welcome us to the neighborhood.

Only minutes have passed from the time we heard pounding on the bedroom door, but it seems like hours.

Whoever banged on the bedroom door seems large and powerful, but Charles bravely swings the bedroom door open.

No one is in the hall—neither did we hear footsteps indicating that they have left. We are still apprehensive, because they may be hiding somewhere, ready to attack us.

Charles and I decide to search the house together. We look everywhere but can't find anyone in the house. We don't think to check the attic. Neither of us would have been brave enough to go up there anyway.

We check all the windows and doors to make sure they are locked, and we look for signs that would indicate that someone has broken into the house. Everything appears to be secure.

All of us make our way back upstairs, but we are still cautious because we know we heard the footsteps and banging on the door, yet we can't find anything that could have made the noises.

We settle back into bed. A few minutes later we hear loud footsteps stomping up the front stairs again!

Charles jumps out of the bed and quickly swings the bedroom door open just as the children run back to our bedroom through the connecting door. The hallway is empty.

Dread washes over me when I realize that the thunderous footfalls and tremendous banging cannot be that of a human. I am frightened to think that we have perhaps just experienced something in the supernatural. I am concerned about staying here, because there is a strong sense of evil prevalent in the house.

I am wondering if it was a good idea to move into this house. Perhaps this is why our friends who lived here before us suddenly moved out of the house and far away from here. They may have purposely left that detail out. I am also wondering if there is a vacancy at the nearby hotel, but I know that we have to make the best of this situation.

Whatever banged on our bedroom door seems powerful and threatening. I wonder what other paranormal specters we may encounter if we stay here. There will be no resting in peace in this house.

Ghosts of departed souls may have rattled the chains in the attic, but I don't know what to think of the huge being that bangs on our bedroom door.

I reason that the huge entity is a male, because the stomping and the banging were so forceful. But I also "sense" the presence of a male.

I wonder why he is so angry, and if he is angry with us or if this is typical ghost behavior. I think on these things while drifting off to sleep on this first night in our new home.

Morning arrives, and the bright sun shines through the windows. It is so peaceful in the mansion that I wonder if all of the unusual things that happened last night were just a bad dream. Unfortunately, I know they were real.

All of my past experiences have not prepared me for this. We have witnessed several manifestations on the first night living in the mansion.

Later we find out that other families who moved into the mansion before we did hadn't stayed for very long because of the kinds of things we endured last night. Some of the families left on the first night of moving in. But we survived our first night in the mansion, and we plan to stay in the home we fell in love with.

The day goes by quickly. We get ready for bed and turn the lights off. Minutes later, the sound of heavy boots and banging on our bedroom door startles us and sends the children running into our bedroom!

Charles quickly jumps out of bed and swings the door open, but he sees no one in the hall.

Charles and I wonder if we should move from this place. We discuss our options and realize that we can't move at this time. Plus, even with the unusual things that are happening, all of us like it here, and so we decide to remain in the mansion.

The spirit haunting us doesn't seem to like this idea, and he bangs on our bedroom door in intervals most of the night. He seems to be trying to get rid of us.

The children don't want to sleep in their bedroom, and I don't blame them. We let them sleep in our bedroom again tonight, and plan to let them sleep in our room every night. There is plenty of space on the floor for their mattresses, and it is comforting to know they are near us.

I was hoping this would be the end of the strange goings on in the house, but I find out that it is just the beginning of a new kind of life we have chosen to live because we have decided to stay in the mansion.

Morning brings with it a new day. I still feel uneasy about the things that happened during the last two nights, but I push these thoughts aside as we enjoy a hearty breakfast. Then everyone goes in different directions downstairs while I wash the dishes.

I walk back through the dining room, but I abruptly stop when I hear the familiar *Boom! Boom! Boom!* of loud footsteps. But this time the ghost stomps down the front stairs and toward us!

I look that way but don't see anything there. The ghost sounds angry, and he seems to be trying to threaten us or frighten us away.

The loud footsteps continue down the hall as the ghost gets closer and closer to us. I know my family hears it, too, because they are quickly coming into the dining room. We feel safer in this room because there is a back door we can run out of if we need to.

We stay close together by the dining room door for a few minutes, and we watch with anticipation to see what the ghost may do.

The footsteps seem to stop at the threshold of the living room, as if the ghost is standing there watching us. We haven't experienced the ghost doing this before. We are only about eight feet away from where he is. We can't see him, but we know he is there.

I can feel his angry eyes boring through me. An uneasy feeling erupts in my soul.

Soon the presence fades, and the house grows quiet again. But we sit silently at the dining room table and anxiously wait to see what else may take place.

We are relieved when nothing else unusual happens, and we talk about other things to get our minds off of what is taking place in our home. Then we decide that if the ghost wants to hang around downstairs, we will go outside for a while. All of us head for the door.

Night comes again, and we settle into bed on our third night of living in the mansion. We expect it to be like the other nights.

We turn the light off and wait to see what happens, and we listen for the sounds that usually come. But the house remains quiet. Nothing unusual happens tonight…but tomorrow night promises the unexpected.

Shannon and Stephen are lying on their mattresses in our room. The hall door is closed, but the door to our children's room is open.

Stephen casually looks into the children's bedroom and is terrified when he sees the man ghost standing in the doorway glaring at him!

He turns to Shannon and whispers, "I see the ghost! He's in our bedroom!" Stephen looks back at the doorway, and the ghost is gone.

I am alarmed when I hear what Stephen whispers to Shannon. I want to protect them but wonder how we can defend ourselves against something unseen. I pray and ask God to protect us.

The ghost might be standing at the doorway in exasperation as he tries to figure out a way to get rid of us. Everything he has tried so far hasn't worked. Maybe the ghost has reasoned that if he can't scare us away, he will try to frighten the children.

Stephen doesn't tell us what the ghost looks like, and none of us think to ask him.

(While writing this book twenty five years later, I ask Stephen if he remembers what the ghost looked like. I am surprised when he is able to vividly recall that childhood memory. He describes the ghost as being huge—about eight feet tall. This is probably why it made such a thunderous noise when it walked. He says that the apparition looked like a black shadow in the shape of a man, and his eyes shone like flashlights where his head should have been. He adds that there were no facial features.)

We lay quietly for a while. Each one of us is absorbed in our own thoughts. All eyes are on the children's bedroom door as we wait to see if the ghost comes into our bedroom.

Nothing else happens tonight that we know of. The house is quiet, and everyone drifts off to sleep. When I open my eyes I realize it is morning.

The presence of the ghost is menacing. He continues to stomp up the front staircase almost every night, and he stomps down the same staircase almost every day of the four years we live in the mansion. The days he appears are sporadic. He almost always comes when we least expect it.

Sometimes Shannon sees the shadow of the man ghost in the downstairs hall.

The man ghost pounds on our bedroom door almost every night. He bangs three times, and then the house gets quiet. We ignore it. About ten minutes later he bangs on the door again.

At times the episodes gradually stop, but usually the cycle continues until one of us gets up and opens the door.

I wonder if the man ghost has done these things to other people who lived in the mansion before us, or if he is just doing this to us. Later we find out that we aren't the only ones who have had such encounters with this huge entity.

The menacing ghost is always stomping and getting angry. He may have done this when he was alive. The ghost may be trying to control everyone in the mansion because he thinks it is still his home and that we are the intruders.

Some murders, suicides, and other tragic deaths seem to cause paranormal activities at the place where the deaths occur. These spirits seem to linger in the areas of the event, thus manifesting in haunting activity.

Someone dabbling in occult practices can open doors to the spiritual realm and give demons authority to be in certain areas. These demons have been given the spiritual ground by which they stand firm on. Whatever is on that land can also be affected. The Bible warns about such things and says to stay away from these practices.

A lot of the slaves that came over through the Caribbean to America were steeped in the practice of voodoo and used it against their cruel masters.

Slaves would communicate with each other and had a silent network of domestics. This caused the slave owners to be more ruthless in order to control their slaves. They would chain them or tie them up to keep tight control of them or to prevent them from running away.

The slaves would resist and spread rumors about the masters. The masters began keeping the slaves from congregating so they wouldn't talk about them or make plans.

Sometimes slaves would perform acts of sabotage to strike back and make things more difficult for the owner. The slaves rebelled because they had been kidnapped from their land and were being mistreated. They were not accustomed to this sort of cruelty.

When I go into the attic one day to put rat poison in it, I am not surprised when I come across three sets of heavy chains attached to the bottom of the two outer walls.

Each chain has a metal band on the end of it. The slaves' feet were probably chained to the attic walls years ago by these ankle bands. My heart sinks with such thoughts, and I don't hang around in the attic to explore any further.

This may explain why we heard chains rattling in the attic on our first night living in the mansion. We hear the chains move around many other times while living in the mansion.

Those slaves had to endure a lot of hardships just being in the attic. It is not known how long the periods of time were that they had to stay up there, but it must have been tortuous for them.

The blistering heat of the roof right above them could have killed them. They also may have suffocated from the closed-in space they were forced to remain in. That was in the summer months. In the winter, there was no source of heat coming into the attic. They may have frozen to death if forced to stay in there for very long.

Perhaps the spirits of some of the slaves remain in the house and in the attic. Later we discover that the small house in the back yard was the slave quarters. We come to realize that it, too, is haunted.

I often have an eerie feeling when I go into that house to wash clothes. Once in a while I notice the washing machine lid has been raised up in the middle of the wash cycle. I wonder if it is the ghost of a slave doing it.

It may have been the ghost of a slave who washed our dishes the first night we lived in the house. The slave may have wanted to avoid the wrath of the man ghost, who may have been her master when they were living in the mansion many years ago. The slave may have got a beating if dishes were left unwashed.

A WOMAN GHOST

While these things are going on in and around the mansion, other unusual events are taking place. Shannon likes to sit on the wooden fence at the edge of the front yard. Sometimes she looks up at our upstairs bedroom window and sees the ghost of an old woman looking back at her!

Sometimes Shannon's friend is with her, and they both see the ghost at the same window. Neighbors and other people passing by say they can see the apparition, not knowing about Shannon and her friend seeing it. The woman ghost appears at the window once in a while. She looks sad and seems to be looking out at the river. The woman ghost is just as unpredictable as the man ghost is when he appears.

The spirit of the old woman inhabits the mansion. She is constantly doting over the care of the house. This is the place she spent many years taking care of. She seems to be bothered by those in the flesh messing with what she thinks is still hers.

Things around the house are often moved out of their place or disappear and are never found. I wonder if the woman ghost is the one doing this.

In the old days, a woman was responsible for the welfare of the home. A husband would chastise his wife if things were not managed. This could be why the woman ghost seems to want us to have everything neatly in its place at all times, or she could have been a neat freak when she was alive and continues to be so now.

I keep our home clean and organized, but with busy lives and young children in the house it is easy for things to get out of place.

This seems to stir the woman ghost up, and she gets active in the house. A woman's work is never done, even for a dead one.

The woman ghost is controlling, and she seems to want our children well behaved at all times. One day Shannon and Stephen decide to play a board game in the day room downstairs. Soon they start arguing. I am entering the room to take care of the situation when suddenly an unseen hand slaps the back of the leather couch!

We watch as the hand print stays indented in the couch for a few seconds, as if the woman ghost is still pressing her hand down into the couch. Then it gradually disappears. At least she didn't slap the children!

Shannon and Stephen get along well after this happens. (Other parents may want to borrow the ghost for a while.)

The ghostly spirits seem to be aware of us, yet are still stuck in their time of when they were alive. Sometimes their time period crosses over into our time.

They are invisible to us most of the time, but they can physically touch things in the house. They seem to be trying to finish something they didn't get to do when they were alive.

SECOND FLOOR EXILE

We have been living in the mansion for a few months, and we still can't get much rest because of the man ghost banging on our bedroom door almost every night.

We decide to move our bedroom downstairs, and we put the children's mattresses in the living room for them to sleep on until we can buy them a day bed with a trundle bed underneath. We hope that by not being in the area where the man ghost haunts, he will leave us alone. We soon realize that he haunts the downstairs, too. He just manifests in different ways.

After moving downstairs, we realize that we also have the old woman ghost to deal with. The room we sleep in now is one of the other areas of the house that she haunts and where my rocking chair is that she often sits in.

We get into bed on our first night sleeping downstairs. The house is quiet as the lights are turned off. We anxiously wait to see what may happen in this new sleeping arrangement.

*Haunted House
of the Rising Sun*

I feel uneasy when I realize that there isn't a door to keep the man ghost from coming into the rooms we sleep in. Then again, he may have been able to go through the walls or door upstairs and was just playing tricks on us by making us think he couldn't. Nevertheless, it made me feel like we were safe by having the door closed. Now I'm not sure I like our new sleeping arrangements.

A few minutes later we hear something we don't expect. There is loud banging on each one of the twenty-three windows of the mansion! There are three loud knocks on a window upstairs, then a few seconds later there are three loud knocks on the next window, and so on, until all of the windows around the house are hit. Then each window downstairs is hit.

We wonder if someone is playing a prank on us. Then we realize there is no way a human could reach the upstairs windows without a very tall ladder—or be able to knock on all of the windows that quickly.

All twenty-three windows in the house are hit in just a few minutes. At least this is better than the loud pounding on our upstairs bedroom was.

The man ghost is probably angry because we moved downstairs instead of moving out of the house. He may be hitting the windows to scare us or to get us to move from the mansion. His plan isn't working. We love living here, and we plan to stay. The ghost finally gives up—for tonight anyway. He may be sulking in a corner, devising a new plan to try and frighten us away.

It never occurs to us to try to take photos of the ghosts, but I happen to catch what appears to be an image of the man ghost on the wall behind Stephen while taking a photo of him opening a

Christmas present by the mattresses in the living room. When the picture is blown up to a larger size, a strange gray haze appears to float above Stephen. I didn't notice the ghostly image until I looked at the photo years later.

Stephen opening a Christmas present by the mattresses in the living room.

I did happen to catch the image of the man ghost with a movie camera. during one of Shannon's middle school band recitals. Regretfully, the VHS tape was destroyed during Hurricane Katrina.

*Haunted House
of the Rising Sun*

After being downstairs for a few weeks, we buy a day bed and trundle bed for Shannon and Stephen to sleep in. The day bed fits perfect in the large living room, and the trundle bed slides under it. The children like their new beds. They can lay in them while watching television, and it gives us more room to sit.

Stephen by the day bed.

The spirits become more active as time goes by, and we rearrange the living room so we can put the children's beds against the wall that divides our bedroom and the living room. Shannon and Stephen don't like sleeping by the window, and I like having the children closer to us.

Shannon & Stephen playing cars in the living room.

THE BOY GHOST

There is a boy ghost that is about six years old in the mansion. He is around the same age as Stephen. The ghost is funny most of the time, and he seems to play much like any kid would.

He likes Shannon and Stephen's toys. Once in a while some of them are mysteriously moved to another room of the house. Other times toys vanish and are never found. They must be the boy's favorite ones.

Once in a while we discover other things missing, and we later find them in a different area of the house. Sometimes they are never found.

Haunted House
of the Rising Sun

It could be the old woman ghost moving some of the things around. She may want to put things where she wants them to be. The ghost could be attempting to impose its will over that of the living. Other times it may be the boy ghost playing one of his pranks on us. I wonder if the spirits actually use the items they take.

Sometimes when we find our children's toys scattered around on the floor, it seems like the boy ghost is just playing with them. We would think rats are doing it, except that we see building blocks stacked up neatly or toy cars lined up in a straight line as if a child had been playing with them.

The television goes off from time to time without anyone touching it. Sometimes the television comes on by itself. It could be the boy ghost doing it. We never had trouble with this television before moving to the mansion or after moving out of it.

Poltergeist activity is the spiritual acting upon the physical. Some would describe such an activity as an invisible entity moving things around or making noises. This could be a cross over in dimensions. Maybe it is a matter of "their time" intruding into our current time.

Sometimes we hear the boy ghost pull the spring on the back door in the kitchen, and then we hear the "boing" of the spring as it is released.

Again and again the spring hits against the screen door. Laughter follows as the boy is amused by it. We laugh, too, because he seems to be having a great time. Sometimes Shannon's friend is in the house and hears it.

One day we are in the dining room and hear the spring reverberating on the open back door. Shannon and I decide to peek in the kitchen to see if we can see the boy. We don't see the boy, but we do see the spring move by itself as it is being released!

Our cats seem to be tuned in to the spirits, and at times they respond to the ghostly behavior. One day we hear all of our cats meowing at the open back door. The cats usually don't come to the door unless someone calls them. We have fed them already, so there is no reason for them to be acting this way.

Shannon and I peek into the kitchen and see all eight cats at the door. The mother to six of them has climbed halfway up the screen door, and she meows as she tries to get inside the house. Among the sounds of the cats is the clear voice of the boy ghost as he calls out to them, "Here, kitty-kitty!"

The cats don't seem afraid or alarmed by the boy ghost. They are trying to come to him at the back door. They probably think he will feed them.

Often the boy ghost follows me around the house as I do chores. It happens most of the time when I am alone in the house.

Once in a while, when I turn directions quickly, I seem to bump into the boy. I can't see him or anything that could have touched me, but I can feel a light pressure like someone bumped into me. Then I hear a soft "ugh" sound, followed by a small thump on the floor, as if the boy had fallen down.

Other times I feel a tug on my clothes and hear a young boy say, "Mommy." This is something my own children do when they want or need something.

When this happens I look down out of instinct to see my clothes being pulled out ever so gently, like a child would do. I don't answer the plea, but just stand still until the boy lets go of me a few seconds later. Then I go about doing my cleaning.

I don't want to give the ghost any attention, and it is unnerving having him around me. I don't sense an evil presence when the boy ghost is around, but I don't like a spirit of any kind near me.

I question why this spirit would identify with me or call me mommy. Do I look similar to or remind his of his mother when she was alive?

In retrospect of everything that is going on in the mansion, I wonder if it is the innocent spirit of a deceased boy or the cunning trick of an evil spirit.

We never speak to the spirits, and we try to ignore them as we attempt to move on with our own lives, but things continue to happen that pull us back into having to deal with the supernatural again.

Three graves are discovered in the area between the mansion and the small slave quarters not long after we move out of the mansion.

There is a mystery regarding who was buried in those graves. It may be the man, woman, and young boy whose ghostly spirits still reside in the mansion.

Some of the deceased seem to haunt the place where they died or where their body is buried. I wonder if there are other unmarked graves in the yard, yet to be discovered. Slaves might be buried there.

A WELCOMED VISITOR

Our assistant pastor, Andrew Cook, comes to see us once in a while and to pray for us. I expect the spirits to act up when he is in the house, but they don't. I am glad the visits are good ones.

During one of his visits, Reverend Cook tells us of an out-of-body experience that occurred to him years ago. He says that he was a master mechanic and director for the Amtrak Railroad at that time. He was superintendent of a wrecking crew of one hundred and twenty men for three weeks, putting in sixteen hour days, working from three p.m. to seven a.m.

In addition to that job, he owned a shipyard and was building 50- to 100-foot long boats. Reverend Cook was also president of two labor unions and involved in ministries. He was a very busy man, but he always made time for his wife and children.

Reverend Cook and his crew were rebuilding a railroad car for then President Carter, whose railroad car had derailed and wrecked. Reverend Cook was an overseer on the project and had the crew working on it night and day.

To keep the work ongoing, Reverend Cook had a caterer prepare food for the men to eat, and had beds available for them to sleep in. When they got their rest, they would go back to work.

Reverend Cook got to rest, but was still very tired when he headed home on this particular night. His wife was already in bed.

He collapsed beside her and was lying on his back. Suddenly he found himself above the bed looking down at his body lying in the bed! His spirit-man had left his body.

Then unexpectedly he found himself walking in a tunnel with Jesus. He was at perfect peace as he walked with Jesus toward a bright light at the end of the tunnel.

Many hands of what he believes to be demons were grabbing at him from both sides of this tunnel, but they could not touch him. They seemed to be trying to stop him from going where he was headed, which was heaven.

Either they were attached to the wall or there was some kind of invisible barrier stopping them from reaching Reverend Cook. Somehow he knew they were not good spirits.

While they were walking through the tunnel, Jesus asked Reverend Cook, "Do you want to go to heaven? Are you ready?"

Then Jesus asked him, "Do you want to go back?" Reverend Cook didn't give a verbal answer, but he thought about his young children that would be fatherless if he died.

Jesus knew his thoughts, and at that moment Reverend Cook began floating back toward his body. He looked down and could see his body lying on the bed as he approached it. Then his spirit went back into his body. He wasn't afraid during the entire experience.

Reverend Andrew Cook

We stay busy and don't dwell on the paranormal phenomena that are happening around us. Despite all that takes place in the mansion, we love living here, and we do fun things as we make the best of the situation.

Shannon and Stephen, ready to play.

The children have plenty of things to do as they hang out in the large yard. They play with our animals or with neighborhood friends. They also hang out in their playhouse and in the trees, but these things don't keep them away from one of the haunting entities.

*Haunted House
of the Rising Sun*

*Our family playing a board game.
(My husband is playing, too, but he took the photograph.)*

Once in a while the children gasp when they see the spirit of a young woman in the loft of the open carriage house by their playhouse!

*Shannon, the cat, and the hamster,
with the carriage house in the background.*

One day Shannon is upset when she runs to tell me that she saw a young woman hanging from a rope in the tree behind the play house! I ask her to show me.

Both of us return to the tree, but we see that no one is there. No signs of a hanging are present.

I wonder if it is the ghost of the young woman the children see in the loft, and if she is buried in this area of the mansion grounds.

A HAUNTED SHIP

We decide to take a break from the stress created by all of the ghostly phenomena going on in the mansion, and we welcome a change of scenery as we visit the USS *Alabama*. The ship is at its final resting place as it sits overlooking Mobile Bay.

The first thing I see upon arrival is the massive battleship rising high above the water. The ship looks like a huge gray floating city. It was self-contained and had everything needed to house hundreds of men. In many ways it was like a city.

We enjoy strolling around and looking at the many static displays of planes, tanks, and other military wares that are scattered around the memorial park. These pieces of military history are a reminder of the terrors and tragedies of war. Many somber memories haunt those soldiers and loved ones who have experienced such things.

The courageous spirits of the men are still in every part of the history of the USS *Alabama*. Ghosts of some of the men still haunt the tools, machines, and walls of the ship, refusing to let them go as they are forever on duty, forever vigilant, and never finding rest.

Visitors of this ship that is now a tourist attraction have seen or heard manifestations of the ghosts of these men who seem to be stuck in time. They have heard the heavy doors of the bulk heads being closed while no one is near them, as well as other noises from the dead ship.

These are ghostly sounds of the deceased men that stay busy about the ship and haunt the very halls they were accustomed to.

Nothing seems to be more horrifying than to die in war, but perhaps even more tragic is to die at the hands of your own comrades. Such an event happened at gun turret number five.

Eight sailors were killed at gun mount number five by gunfire from gun mount number nine when the safety feature failed to work. The rain of ordinance at close range disintegrated their bodies. This did not leave much for a proper burial.

The ship's crew probably carried with them the guilt of the senseless loss of their crew mates.

We are unaware of these events as we board the permanently docked ship for a walking tour with all of the other tourists from near and far.

Our children are excited, and they ask engaging questions about the equipment they encounter as we enter each room of the ship.

We are intrigued as we walk up and down the decks and into the many compartments to see how the men worked and lived on this huge battleship. We view the radio room, sick bay, and many other departments. They each have a function, like the organs of a body, and they bring the ship to life.

While viewing one of the turrets, I start having the strange feeling that humans aren't the only ones on board with us. I suddenly feel sadness in this area of the ship.

Soon Shannon makes a few comments about feeling an eerie presence and states that she is ready to leave. This surprises me, because Shannon was very interested in the ship just a few minutes ago. But I understand why she wants to go. I have an unsettling feeling about being here, too.

When we get to the officer's room of the ship, Shannon starts looking nervous and doesn't want to go near it. I am interested in viewing the room but also feel apprehensive about it.

Charles and Stephen don't seem to notice anything out of the ordinary.

I stick my head in the officer's room and have a quick look, but I have a feeling that someone is watching me.

The eerie presence continues to pervade the place. Goose bumps gather on my arms, and the hairs on my neck stand out. I get a strong feeling that we should leave.

A few seconds later Shannon says in a serious tone, "I want to leave. Now." The tour is near its end, anyway. We make our way down the gangway and head to the nearby gift shop to look around.

We are in the gift shop for only a few minutes when I start having the same eerie feeling I had while on the ship. I also get the feeling that someone is intensely watching us.

Then without warning, a few glass souvenirs fly off of the shelf in front of me! They crash onto the floor by my feet. It is as if someone angrily swung their hand across the shelf.

I sense that it is the same unseen entity Shannon and I encountered when we were on the ship. It must have followed us into the gift shop. I am thinking, *Oh, no, not again*. We came here to get away from ghosts, and now one is bothering us here.

Then I begin to wonder if a ghost from our house followed us here. What a way to live, wondering if ghosts are stalking us when we leave the house.

My thoughts are interrupted by other things flying off of the shelf near Shannon! I am getting concerned now and am wondering if we are in danger. The ghosts at our house don't do things like this. The young cashier hears the crash this time, and casually says, "Don't worry about it. This happens all the time. It is a ghost that comes in here from the ship."

I am surprised that the cashier knows what is happening, and I am glad we aren't the only ones experiencing the paranormal phenomena. I feel sorry for the girl. She has to clean up the messes the ghost makes. It is a strange feeling to be glad when we return to our haunted mansion. We can't seem to get away from ghosts.

I return to the USS *Alabama* several years later with my second husband, Steve Till, and his two children, Kellie and Stevie. I am a little nervous as we pull into the parking lot, and I can't believe that I am returning to the place where frightening memories of days gone by still haunt me. I haven't told Steve or his children about the ghostly encounters I had on my last trip here. I push these thoughts aside as we exit our van, and I am determined to have a good time while here.

We have fun walking around and viewing the many displays of planes and other items of war on the memorial park grounds. We take photos of us clowning around as we advance from one display to the next. Touching the equipment brings history to life.

I am glad that touring the ship isn't in our plans today. We were just passing through the area and have stopped for a short visit. I haven't told them about any of my past ghost encounters, and I don't want to have any today. We don't have any paranormal experiences while here, but that could be because we didn't tour the ship. I share the previous ghost encounters of the ship and gift shop on the way to our next destination, a Florida beach.

Bringing up the subject of ghosts makes Kellie feel comfortable enough with me to later share some of the paranormal phenomena she has had in their home over the years, in the house I recently moved into with them.

The USS Alabama. Stevie and Kellie in the back, me in the front.

THE MANSION INSPIRED A SONG

A knock on our front door brings with it unexpected information about a piece of history regarding the mansion. Three older gentlemen standing on our front porch introduce themselves as members of the original band who played the song "House of the Rising Sun"!

They tell us that the composer of that song wrote it while sitting in the dining room of the mansion. We follow one of the men into the dining room, and he shares the story with us.

There had been a party one night. The gentleman pointed to one of the windows in the dining room, saying that the composer had looked out of that window the next morning and watched the sun rise over the river as he wrote the song. This could mean that he penned the lyrics or that he composed the music.

The view is serene as you look out of that window and watch the sun rising over the river.

The hauntings that took place in the mansion hint of an unsavory past that coincide with the lyrics of the song. The men claimed that the mansion we reside in is the "house of the rising sun."

Later this famous song became an inspiration for the front cover of my first published ghost book, *Haunted House of the Rising Sun*.

Upon leaving, the nice gentleman expressed his appreciation for being able to enter the house. He was grateful to be able to touch a piece of their past.

I wonder if recalling events of their past will haunt his memories, especially if they had any paranormal experiences while here. The other two men looked nervous and didn't want to come into the house. They had made haste back to their automobile when the other gentleman mentioned going into the mansion.

SHANNON ALMOST IN A MOVIE

The movie *Interview with the Vampire: the Vampire Chronicles*, starring Tom Cruise, Brad Pitt, Antonio Banderas, Stephen Rea, and Christian Slater was filmed near the mansion. Shannon was picked to be an extra actor in the movie. Upon her arrival, Shannon was told to wait and see if the girl who was supposed to play the part showed up. If the girl was late getting there, then Shannon would get the part. The girl showed up three minutes before the shooting of the scene began.

Shannon didn't get the part, but she did get to walk around on the set and eat at the buffet table. She had a great time.

She wanted to watch when the set was burned down at the end of shooting the movie, but she was out of town with me at the time. It must have been a spectacular scene as the blaze shot into the sky on the levee near the mansion we had lived in.

SHANNON AN EXTRA CAST MEMBER

In 2011, Shannon is speaking to my nephew Eliot on Facebook, when he mentions a movie for which he is an extra cast member. Half joking, Shannon asks him if there is a part for her.

Her heart leaps with joy when Eliot gives her a list of acting companies she can apply to. She is very grateful to him for giving her this opportunity. For many years now, Shannon has wanted to do this.

An hour after applying online for the part as an extra cast member, Shannon gets a reply! Thanks to Eliot, Shannon gets to be an extra actor in the last episode of *Treme*. *Treme* is an HBO television series about New Orleans after Hurricane Katrina, and this scene is filmed in the French Quarter.

It is an exciting day for Shannon, as she slips on an elegant dark blue dress and meets the cast she will be working with. She has a great time and gets to eat at a fancy restaurant.

Shannon in her blue dress.

Chapter 12

Can't Get Away From Spirits

Stephen and I.

We are relieved when we finally get to move out of the mansion and away from the spirits who reside here. But there is also sadness about leaving the house we have come to love.

I like the three-bedroom house our real estate agent shows us, but I wonder why there is just a cement slab in the back yard where a shed once stood. Then I realize the house must have flooded during one of the past hurricanes. I don't say anything to Charles about it, because I know we can't be too picky with the low price range we have to work with.

Then I notice an unusual red stain on the light-colored linoleum floor in front of the kitchen sink. It resembles blood stains. It is as if someone was cut and a few small puddles of blood collected on the floor. Small droplets of red are scattered around it. I hope the stain is just spilled fingernail polish or some other household liquid.

The red spots look fresh, as if it happened recently. This puzzles me, because no one is occupying the house at this time. It looks as if no one has lived here for a while. I believe the real estate agent would disclose to us if someone had died in the house, if she knew about it. Death of the owner may be why it is for sale.

I don't want a stain on the floor to deter us from buying the house, so I don't say anything about it. Later I wish I had asked the real estate agent about it.

We decide to buy the house, and we begin moving into it. Among our things is the antique cedar robe we had purchased from the previous renters of the mansion.

We don't think about the vision Shannon saw of a child's skull in the cedar robe. (This story is told in detail in my book, *Haunted House of the Rising Sun.*) We put the cedar robe in the living room to use for our coats and extra blankets. It sits against the wall near the kitchen. Nor do we think that something sinister may happen by bringing the cedar robe to this house.

We get settled into our new residence, which is not far from the haunted mansion we just moved out of.

Shannon and Stephen like having their own bedrooms, and they are glad that they attend the same school they were going to before the move. Things are looking better for us. Our hope is that this is the right place and the final move for us.

But something frightening happens within the first week of moving into the house.

Shannon and Stephen in our back yard.

I am alone in the house after Charles leaves for work, and the children get on the school bus.

The karaoke is blasting out one of my favorite songs as I sing along with it. The window shades are up to welcome the bright sunlight in while I wash the breakfast dishes.

I am almost finished washing the dishes when I begin to feel something lightly brush against the top of my left foot. I am thinking that one of my long hairs fell on my foot, or that a bug is on my foot. Without looking, I brush my foot with the other foot and continue washing the dishes.

A few minutes later I feel it again. I look down, but nothing is there that I can see. The only thing I notice is that my left foot is on the mysterious red stain.

All of a sudden I get an eerie feeling that someone is watching me. I also have the distinct feeling that the mysterious red stain on the floor has something to do with the evil presence now pervading the room.

I think, *Oh no, not again,* as I remember the paranormal things that have happened in other homes I lived in. A dread comes over me when I realize that I have to stand in this spot every day to prepare meals and wash dishes. I can't seem to get away from spirits. The excitement of living here diminishes with these thoughts. I start praying for God to protect me and my family.

All of my past experiences with the paranormal should have prepared me for what happens next, but they don't.

The pressure of something brushing across my foot becomes a little harder, and it feels like an unseen being stroking their long, sharp fingernails back and forth along the top of my foot! I become aware that something paranormal is happening.

Fear pushes its way into my peaceful morning, and goose bumps rise upon my flesh. Prayers for protection increase as I continue washing the dishes. I am determined to go on with my usual routine and not let the plans of uninvited spirits interrupt my life.

A few minutes later, when I move over a little to rinse the dishes in the other sink, my right foot shifts onto the red stain.

Suddenly I feel the invisible specter scratching my right foot! It is like the spirit is intimidating and taunting me.

The threatening strokes begin to slowly ascend up my ankle! This frightens me, and I get nervous about what else the spirit may do. My prayers shift as I ask God to send angels to help me, and I begin rebuking the evil spirit. After engaging in spiritual warfare for several minutes, the spirit finally leaves.

I breathe a sigh of relief and thank God for helping me during this ordeal. Then I finish rinsing the dishes. The house feels peaceful again, but it isn't the only encounter I have with this being.

Every now and then I feel the same sensation of long fingernails stroking my foot while washing the dishes. At first I try to ignore the spirit, but it doesn't leave until I pray and rebuke it in Jesus' name.

The only time I feel this strange sensation is while standing on the red stain in the kitchen. Sometimes it happens when my family is in the house. No one has mentioned that they feel the strange scratching, but they don't stand by the sink as long as I do. I don't say anything to my family about it. I don't want them to worry, if this is the only unusual thing that happens in the house.

Then other strange things begin to happen in our home. Items begin to disappear and are found in other parts of the house. Sometimes they are never found.

I am wondering if a spirit followed us here from the haunted mansion we just moved out of. When we brought the old cedar robe here from the mansion, a spirit may have come with it. But the spirit who scratches my feet seems to be different than the ones we encountered in the mansion. Then I wonder if the spirit is here because someone died or was murdered in this kitchen. There may be more than one spirit invading our home.

It is good that we have busy schedules that get us out of the house. I am a substitute teacher, and I work almost every day. Shannon is in band at school, and Stephen is on the neighborhood basketball team. We go to the local park often, and we attend church at least three times a week.

Shannon and I sing at church, and she helps me with the puppets as I teach children's church. She also works in the nursery with the babies.

But gradually Shannon loses interest in spiritual growth, and she doesn't want to attend church anymore. She becomes interested in dark things and starts reading the type of books I disapprove of.

Then something frightening happens to Shannon. She is sound asleep one night when something shakes her and wakes her up. Shannon thinks it is one of us.

She opens her eyes and freaks out when she sees a skeleton face only a few inches from her face! She can see it well because of the hall light shining into her bedroom.

Shannon quickly throws the covers over her head as she shakes with fear. Her heart beats wildly as she peeks out from under the covers a few minutes later to see if the terrifying face is still there. She is relieved when she realizes that it is gone, but she stays awake most of the night wondering if it will return.

Shannon tells us about her horrible ordeal the next morning. After Charles leaves for work and the children go to school, I pray most of the day for God's protection and deliverance for my family and myself.

A few months later, Shannon wakes up to see several demons standing around her bed! She is terrified and throws the covers over her head. When she peeks out a few minutes later, she sees that they are gone, but she stays awake most of the night out of fear that they may return.

She tells me about the terrifying experience the next morning. I tell Shannon, "You should have come to get me."

She says, "I was too afraid to move."

Then I tell her, "You could have called out to me." I would have been there within seconds. Our bedroom is on the other side of the wall from hers.

Shannon answers, "I was too scared to speak."

Shannon may be inviting demons into our home through the dark things she is involved in, or the spirits may have been in the house when we moved into it.

One of the entities that is manifesting to Shannon, and later to Stephen, might be the same one who scratches my feet. I continue doing spiritual warfare, and I ask Christian friends to pray for us.

Stephen meets new friends and begins drifting away from his strong faith in God.

I continue teaching our children the Bible at church and at home, and I pray with them at bedtime and when needed. Stephen still likes that I read him Bible stories each night upon going to bed.

One night, I have a dream of Stephen and his best friend running through our house playing. Suddenly the boys aren't laughing anymore. They look scared and seem to be running from something.

I look down and see a large snake chasing them! I know it must be poisonous, because Stephen usually isn't afraid of snakes. He keeps one in a tank in his room. I try to get the boys to safety, but they go the other way. Then the snake strikes my son on his ankle! Sorrow fills my heart, because I know that death will probably soon come.

When I wake up from having this frightening dream, I know it has a spiritual significance. I believe that God allowed me to have this dream as a way of telling me to continue praying and doing spiritual warfare for my children.

They seem to be running full force into the world and away from God. Sorrow fills my heart as I see them being led astray, knowing that spiritual death may follow behind it.

Shannon meets new friends at school that are gothic. She wants to fit in with the group, and she becomes more interested in the occult than she is about God.

She borrows tarot cards from a friend, and soon Shannon is able to tell her friends' fortunes. This reminds me of when my mother and sister told peoples' fortunes from the Bible years ago.

Disappointment and fear are usually encountered in the present. The future is uncertain, and regret is always oriented to the past.

Those that want the future revealed desire to get good or favorable reports about whom they may marry or what will happen next in their life. They are trusting in something other than God for their future. It is a fantasy or deep desire that is validated by seducing words.

Fortune telling causes Shannon to have a sense of power over people, and she believes that she has control over their thoughts and actions.

This is witchcraft. Those who practice these sorts of things are walking in darkness. These types of illusions lead Shannon astray. Shannon doesn't realize the spiritual trouble she is getting herself into.

Later Stephen becomes part of the gothic group Shannon is in, and he follows her into some of the darker things in which she is involved.

I have seen people set free and delivered from demonic influences and even demonic possession. This encourages me to continue praying for our children's deliverance.

Shannon and Stephen are inviting evil spirits into our home by the things they are doing. They are giving the demons authority to be here.

A battle ensues. I am casting demons out of our home, and they are inviting the demons back in. Many prayers go up to God for my children.

It is also around this time that my husband becomes more short-tempered and unreasonable. He has always been that way, but during the past few years he has become progressively worse.

We divorce within a year of moving out of the haunted mansion and into this house. I move out of our house with the children, but soon Shannon and Stephen decide to move back there with their father.

Faith in God and embracing his Word gives me strength and keeps me going through these trying times.

The scripture Jeremiah 29:11 says, "For I know the thoughts that I think toward you, saith the Lord, thoughts of peace, and not evil, to give you an expected end."

Satan is attacking me from all directions and soon gets a stronghold in an area of my life that I didn't expect. He takes advantage of a weakness I fail to strengthen. I become discouraged and worn down by the enemy and get drawn back into the same sin I was trapped in years ago.

I continue going to church, and I pray for God to deliver all of us from the clutches of Satan. He has a strong hold on us. I gradually get free from the sin that had me bound and become strong in God again.

I understand how Satan entraps people. Now I am even more determined to get my children out of his clutches.

Hope rises up in me when Shannon, Stephen, and other members of the group want me to start a Bible study at my house for them to attend. But circumstances prevent it from happening. Some of them do visit church once in a while. Spiritual warfare ensues in full force as I intercede for my children and their friends, and claim them back from the enemy.

One day I go to pick up Shannon and Stephen for a visit, and Stephen says he wants to show me something. He lifts up his shirt to reveal a set of long, deep scratches on the center of his stomach! I know that they are from a demon.

Stephen says, "They were there when I woke up this morning." He is a sound sleeper. It didn't wake Stephen up when the demon scratched him.

The demons are stirred up in this house and are probably lashing out because they are afraid of the power of Jesus. They know they will have to leave if Shannon and Stephen come back to God and get set free.

I am angry at the demon who tried to harm my son, and I am more determined than ever to get my children back from the enemy of their souls.

Stephen at 14 with Shannon, 17, in 1997.

Shannon calls me one day and says she wants to come to one of our home Bible studies. I get excited when she returns to God before she leaves our house.

Shannon gets married and starts a family. She has no problems during pregnancy with her first child, Ivy, but there are complications while Shannon is pregnant with her second child, Kurdt. Years later she has the same problems while pregnant with her third child, Dorian. Shannon sees two male angels standing beside her bed during the delivery of both children.

The angels don't say a word, but they give Shannon reassuring smiles as they watch her babies come into the world. Shannon and both of her children have no problems during the deliveries. God sent angels to make sure of that.

Ivy, Dorian, and Kurdt.

Stephen joins the Navy after graduating from high school in 2001. He attends church services while in the Navy, and he finally returns to the God he so loved as a child.

Stephen gets married and moves out of the house at the end of his six-year tour in the Navy. He and Macel serve God and faithfully attend church.

Years later, Shannon contacts some of the members of the gothic group they were involved in, and she learns that they are serving God.

Swamped by Ghosts

Stephen

Macel & Stephen

This chapter has a happy ending because of these things, and because Stephen never has another demonic attack. But Shannon and her family are hurled into frightening paranormal encounters in homes they move into.

Three years after divorcing and moving out of the house, I begin having similar experiences in places where I live. They begin when I remarry and move in with my new husband and his two children. I'm not living there long when I realize that the house is infested with ghosts. Then we have spirit encounters in other homes we move into.

Shannon and Stephen are among those in our family who are the third generation to experience paranormal phenomena, and their children are among those who are the fourth generation to witness such things.

One can only speculate the reason behind paranormal phenomena. I wonder if some of the encounters my family has had throughout the years are actually spirits of our departed relatives. If it is, this makes the encounters not as scary to me.

Some of the spiritual activity may be a result of things we did, what our parents were involved in, or possibly the result of the sins of our ancestors. Then again, we may just happen to live in homes that are haunted.

The spiritual and physical experiences I have had help to prepare me for what is happening in the world today, and for things that are coming. I hope this book helps you in your struggles.

I believe that some of the spiritual encounters I have had were not by chance. They were demonic attacks and a result of choices I made. God used some of the situations to help steer me back into the right spiritual path.

Other experiences were brought about by attacks of Satan because I am a Christian.

We are at the end of the age of man, and Satan knows it. He will use whatever vices he can to draw believers of God back into the world of sin. Spiritual and physical influences are in the world like never before. Evil is ever increasing. The future on earth looks bleak as we come to the end of this age.

Man's only hope is in becoming a born-again believer in Christ Jesus. It doesn't matter what we go through if we belong to God. Whether we live or die as a believer, we are promised eternal life with God. Those who deny Jesus will have no hope.

Chapter 13

Spiritual Activity

I added this last chapter for those who are interested in the spiritual activity that is going on in the world today. Many people have questions about this, and I hope to point them in the right direction for the answers. All scriptures in this book are from the King James Version of the Bible.

As humans we are a spiritual people. Our spirit is who we are. It drives us, inspires us, and is the core of our character. Events take place all around each one of us every moment of every day in the physical world.

Activity is also constantly at work around us in the spiritual realm. There is a spiritual war raging between good and evil, heaven and hell, angels and demons. Though this war is mostly unseen by human eyes, everyone who ever lived on earth is involved in it.

From the time the devil deceived Eve in God's perfect garden, to when Satan will be cast into the lake of fire by God, there is a struggle over the minds and souls of mankind. Satan knows that God wins, but he wants to destroy as many human lives as he can before the end of his era.

At this time in history the war in the spiritual realm is heating up. It is not a time for the uninformed, and those who aren't serving God should reconsider. It is not a time for Christians to be lazy. We are soldiers in this spiritual battle. It is time for us to wake up spiritually and to get ready for what is coming upon the world. It is time to call all Christians to prayer. The intensity of the warfare will increase each day because Jesus is coming soon, and Satan knows it.

Evil today is far greater than it was in the past. The evil in the near future is going to be far greater than it is now. One analogy that can make this clear would be to imagine time as a pregnant woman.

For a long time events would ebb and flow with the tide. However, the further along in time that events unfold, the faster they increase in intensity and the shorter their intervals—just as childbirth labor pains quicken and intensify. As any mother can tell you, the delivery will run its course to its completion. So is it in our time today.

We are faced with the end times. They are going to happen. Whether you like it or not, and if you believe it or not, there is going to be a delivery. It is not as simple as a mother getting a boy or a girl at the end of it. What the world will receive in this delivery is much more, and it is not good.

The most cruel, the most powerful, and the most evil thing to walk the earth is about to enter our world. It is the Antichrist.

Spiritual Activity

With him will be the False Prophet, and Satan himself will join them in a force stronger than any other before them.

These three thoroughly evil beings will make up the unholy trinity. It will be the exact opposite of God's Holy Trinity. With these three beings comprising Satan's forces is one third of the fallen angels that were cast out of heaven with him.

Satan has all of the lost souls who have died without salvation. Included in this massive number, the evil Antichrist will have a growing number of human followers on Earth doing his bidding.

Satan gathers a great army against God, but he loses big time at the end of the battle. Satan already knows it. The question is how much damage will occur until he is taken out of the way by Jesus himself.

The Bible gives us clues to let us know that the end time is near. The end of the age is closer than it ever was before. Jesus gave us signs to indicate the end of the age. Jesus also lets us know that He is coming back soon. Jesus is coming to gather His followers, and He will return again to overthrow the devil and his Antichrist.

SIGNS TO INDICATE THE END OF THE AGE

1. False Christs.

2. False Prophets.

Matthew 24:4-27 states, "And Jesus answered and said unto them, Take heed that no man deceive you. For many shall come in my name, saying, I am Christ; and shall deceive many...And many false prophets shall rise, and shall deceive many...Then if any man shall say unto you, Lo, here is Christ, or there; believe it not. For there shall arise false Christs, and false prophets, and shall shew great signs and wonders; insomuch that, if it were possible, they shall deceive the very elect...Wherefore if they shall say unto you, Behold, he is in the desert; go not forth: behold, he is in the secret chambers; believe it not. For as the lightning cometh out of the east, and shineth even unto the west; so shall also the coming of the Son of man be."

Many people perish due to a lack of knowledge. In the end times there will be lying signs and wonders (Revelations 13:14). Many will be deceived by them.

Those who don't understand what is going on will be faint-hearted, fearful, and may feel overwhelmed by it all. It doesn't have to be this way for the believers in Christ Jesus. The Bible says to fear not, for the Lord is with you. No weapon formed against you will prosper. Greater is Jesus in you than the devil is in the world.

It was so powerful when Jesus was resurrected from the dead that other tombs burst open and many godly men and women who had died came back to life again (Matthew 27: 50-53).

God will gain the final victory, and Satan will be destroyed.

Study the Bible and know it well. Then you will be prepared, and will not succumb to Satan's deceptions. The Bible says that the truth shall set you free.

Test the spirits, and rely on the Holy Spirit to help you. Then you will know whether any teaching you hear agrees with the Bible. The Bible is the truth.

Spiritual Activity

Walk in the spirit. When you are being led by the Holy Spirit, he will make you more sensitive and aware of what is truth and what is error.

1 John 4:1 says, "Beloved, believe not every spirit, but try the spirits whether they are of God; because many false prophets are gone out into the world."

3. Widespread Wars.

4. Famines, Pestilence, & Earthquakes.

Matthew 24:6-8 says, "And ye shall hear of wars and rumours of wars; see that ye be not troubled; for all these things must come to pass, but the end is not yet. For nation shall rise against nation, and kingdom against kingdom: and there shall be famines, and pestilences, and earthquakes, in divers places. All these are the beginning of sorrows."

5. Tribulations & Afflictions.

Matthew 24:9-10 states "Then shall they deliver you up to be afflicted, and shall kill you: and ye shall be hated of all nations for my name's sake. And then shall many be offended, and shall betray one another, and shall hate one another."

6. The Gospel of Jesus Christ Preached Throughout the World.

Matthew 24:14 says, "And this gospel of the kingdom shall be preached in all the world for a witness unto all nations; and then shall the end come."

7. The Holy Spirit Will be Poured Out.

These are God's Administrations of the Holy Spirit: The Spirit of Wisdom, the Spirit of Judgment, the Spirit of Counsel, the Spirit of Might, the Spirit of the Knowledge of God, the Reverence of God, and the Spirit of the Love of God.

God is pouring his spirit upon mankind in an attempt to bring back to him as many people as possible in the last days. God desires that everyone would be saved. He patiently waits, but that time will soon pass, and judgment will be set.

We are already seeing how the earth is being prepared for the coming judgments that God will pour out upon mankind during the Great Tribulation. These judgments are reserved for those who refuse to serve him.

The world is being overrun with godlessness. Cities are filled with drugs and crime. Every kind of sinful and godless behavior is widespread, and at times it is even glorified. It is coming to a town near you. But at this same time revival is spreading throughout the world. People are being set free. It is as if the world itself is being shaken to see which side people will be on; to separate the believers from the non-believers. Many unbelievers will be against those who faithfully serve God. Because if this will come much persecution of the Christians.

2 Timothy 3:1-7 states: "This know also, that in the last days perilous times shall come. For men shall be lovers of their own selves, covetous, boasters, proud, blasphemers, disobedient to parents, unthankful, unholy, without natural affection, trucebreakers, false accusers, incontinent, fierce, despisers of those that are good, traitors, heady, highminded, lovers of pleasures more than lovers of God...ever learning, and never able to come to the knowledge of the truth."

It may look like God is not doing anything about the path the world is on, but he is actually allowing the free will of man to continue in order for each person to decide to come to Him.

All of these things that seem bad are allowed only to bring us to Jesus.

John 14:6 says, "Jesus saith unto him, I am the way, the truth, and the life; no man cometh unto the Father, but by me."

Jesus offers forgiveness and salvation to all that repent and call upon His name. Remember, Jesus wins! Those who belong to Jesus have the Holy Spirit dwelling within them. Our job as Christians is to destroy the works of the devil.

We should share the testimony of our faith in Jesus to those around us. Preachers aren't the only ones who are called to share the gospel of Christ. The Bible says that all Christians should preach the gospel; to be ready at all times to share the good news of the gospel. We can do the same works that Jesus did (John 14:12-13). Jesus defeated sin, death, hell, and Satan, and so can we.

WAYS TO DEFEAT THE DEVIL

- *Walk in obedience.* Make sure you are living right so you will know the will of God concerning you.

- *Submit yourself to God.* Draw close to Him, and He will draw close to you (James 4:8).

- *Resist the devil*...and he will flee from you (James 4:7).

- *Stand on God's Word.* Read the Bible to find out what God promises for His children. Claim those promises for your needs and for your life. Put your faith into action.

- *Proclaim the Word.* Speak God's Word to your need, and to Satan and his demons when they attack. This is what Jesus did.

- ***Walk in faith***. Without faith in God it is impossible to please Him or to defeat the devil. Faith is your invisible shield of protection.

- ***Bind the devil in the name of Jesus***. (Don't attempt this if you don't know how!) Loose the blessings God has for you from Satan's grasp by claiming them back (Matthew 12:28-29 & 16:19).

- ***Stand your ground***...and don't give up no matter what you see or feel. Be brave, be bold. God is on your side. If you are afraid of Satan the enemy, and try to run, he will devour you. If you stand your ground against him, using your weapons of spiritual warfare, he will flee from you.

- ***Pray***. Prayer is powerful! Don't underestimate the power of God through sincere prayer. Pray all the time. The power of prayer changes things, and it changes situations for the better. It activates God to move on your behalf. You have not because you haven't asked for it. Ask, and it will be given to you, if it is according to God's will. Have faith for the answer.

Our nation is removing God from its schools, the government, and other public places, because many want to be "politically correct." It is as if God and Jesus have become words not to be spoken. They are trying to silence the voice of the Christians. But we should never be ashamed of the gospel or to speak the name of the Lord.

Many Christians are falling away from the true faith rather than standing firm on Christian values. Some of them, along with a major portion of society, have embraced the new age thinking. They are falling for the lie by not holding on to the truth. You can and should stand up for what is true and what is good.

Now with the increase in technology and travel, the New World Order is about to take place. The whole world will be controlled by the Antichrist, and the New World Order will be used to do it. That is why there will be a one world government, a one world system, a one world religion, and a one world monetary system. The New World Order is subject to the devil's system, and their goal is to enslave humanity. This has been Satan's plan all along.

Revelation 13:16-17 says, "He causeth all, both small and great, rich and poor, free and bond, to receive a mark in their right hand, or in their foreheads: And that no man might buy or sell, save he that had the mark, or the name of the beast, or the number of his name."

Because of these advances in technology, the globe is a much smaller place. We can easily communicate around the world. Because of this, the Mark of the Beast is able to be implemented.

I caution you, no matter how bad things look, don't take the mark. Look to God instead for your deliverance and salvation. Jesus said that He will never leave you or forsake you if you belong to Him. Don't be dismayed by the things you see. Be ready for the second coming of Jesus Christ. If you are not strong in the faith, get to a spirit-filled, Bible teaching church to learn more.

Since the beginning of time there has been one constant enemy of mankind, and that is the devil. From the Garden of Eden to present day he has always been a foe that is relentless in his attacks on you and me. Satan tricked Adam and Eve and has been lying to people ever since.

Swamped by Ghosts

This master of lies has learned a few things over the years. He has better marketing strategies than ever before. Satan has the majority of the world believing that evil is good, that sin is alright. One of his tricks is in causing people to believe that they will not be held accountable. God rewards those who follow and obey him, but there is punishment for those who follow the lie.

The world as we know it is growing in corruption. Sin abounds in all areas of the world. Evil has spread like a cancer just as the Bible said it would. Most everything today promotes every kind of sin, and devil worship is prevalent in the world.

Everything around us can be used as a vice to try and trick people into thinking that sin is alright. The devil is a liar and a seducer. Either sin will move in and push God out, or the Holy Spirit will move in and push sin out. One will always dominate. This is where your free will comes into play. You have to choose.

God kicked Lucifer and his followers out of heaven and sent them to earth where sin now abounds. They are also bound to a place we call hell. Hell was created by God. He prepared it as a place to send the fallen angels and the devil. This place was kindled from the anger of God when one third of the host of heaven chose to follow Lucifer. They dwell inside the earth.

The devil has been there since that time. He roams the earth, looking for those whom he may devour, then returns to torment those in hell. Hell was not meant for mankind. But every person that denies Christ, and is living in rebellion when they die, chooses to go there.

1 Peter 5:8 says, "Be sober, be vigilant; because your adversary the devil, as a roaring lion, walketh about, seeking whom he may devour."

How does the devil deceive so many people? He has developed tactics over the years to trick and seduce you into sin. It is easy for him because we assist him without realizing it. We become tempted or dissatisfied and do something that we know is contrary to what is right. We know the difference between right and wrong by our conscience, our moral standards, society, and the law of God—but we sin anyway.

Eventually, continual sin progresses into a spiritual bondage and the devil becomes your master. You have given him the authority to wreck havoc in your life. You reap all the consequences of what you have sown. Did you do this alone? No. The devil didn't make you do it, but he influenced you to do wrong. He has evil spirits to help him and weapons in his arsenal to defeat you with. The devil wants you afraid, silent, and powerless.

God uses people to do His work, with the help of the Holy Spirit. Jesus gives us authority in His name to minister to others and to destroy the works of the devil. The Holy Spirit provides us with spiritual Gifts, the Fruits of the Spirit, and tools for spiritual warfare.

The three things the devil cannot fight against is the Word of God, the testimony of your salvation and what Jesus has done for you, and the Holy Spirit. You win!

Mark 16:15 states, "And he [Jesus] said unto them, Go ye into all the world, and preach the gospel to every creature."

God gave us the Ten Commandments to show us right from wrong and how to live as a society. It provides us with a standard to follow.

THE TEN COMMANDMENTS
(*Exodus 20:1-17*)

    I **Thou shalt have no other gods before me**.

   II **Thou shalt not make unto thee any graven image**, or any likeness of any thing that is in heaven above, or that is in the earth beneath, or that is in the water under the earth. Thou shalt not bow down thyself to them, nor serve them; for I the Lord thy God am a jealous God, visiting the iniquity of the fathers upon the children unto the third and fourth generation of them that hate me; And showing mercy unto thousands of them that love me, and keep my commandments.

  III **Thou shalt not take the name of the Lord in vain**; for the Lord will not hold him guiltless that taketh his name in vain.

  IV **Remember the Sabbath day, to keep it holy**. Six days shalt thou labour, and do all thy works; but the seventh day is the Sabbath of the Lord thy God: in it thou shalt not do any work, thou, nor thy son, nor thy daughter, the manservant, nor thy maidservant, nor thy cattle, nor thy stranger that is within thy gates: for in six days the Lord made heaven and earth, the sea, and all that in them is, and rested the seventh day: wherefore the Lord blessed the Sabbath day, and hallowed it.

   V **Honor thy father and thy mother**: that thy days may be long upon the land which the Lord thy God giveth thee.

  VI **Thou shalt not kill**.

VII Thou shalt not commit adultery.

VIII Thou shalt not steal.

IX Thou shalt not bear false witness against thy neighbor.

X Thou shalt not covet anything that belongs to anyone else.

There are two main commandments that are the most important to follow. All of God's commandments fall under these two categories:

Matthew 22:37-40 "Jesus said unto them, Thou shalt love the Lord thy God with all thy heart, and with all thy soul, and with all thy mind. This is the first and great commandment. And the second is like unto it, Thou shalt love thy neighbor as thyself. On these two commandments hang all the law and the prophets."

THINGS THE BIBLE WILL DO

- The Bible discovers and convicts us of sin.
- God's Word helps cleanse us from the pollutions of sin.
- The Bible imparts, strengthens, and instructs us in what we are to do in our daily lives.
- The Bible provides us with a spiritual sword for victory over sin and makes our lives fruitful.
- God's Word gives us power in prayer.

The gift of salvation is free to us if we ask for it. The point at which we confess our sins to Jesus and ask Him to come into our heart is the point of conversion. Our spirit is born and the Holy Spirit moves in. We now have the tools and desire to live holy. It is not our righteousness, but the righteousness of Jesus that we claim and put on.

Romans 10:8-13 says, "But what saith it? The word is nigh thee, even in thy mouth, and in thy heart: that is, the word of faith, which we preach; That if thou shalt confess with thy mouth the Lord Jesus, and shalt believe in thine heart that God hath raised him from the dead, thou shalt be saved. For with the heart man believeth unto righteousness; and with the mouth confession is made unto salvation. For the scripture saith, whosoever believeth on him shall not be ashamed. For there is no difference between the Jew and the Greek: for the same Lord over all is rich unto all that call upon him. For whosoever shall call upon the name of the Lord shall be saved."

If you don't know the Lord Jesus Christ as your personal savior and want to, pray the prayer below or a similar prayer that comes from your heart. Talk to God the same way you talk to family and friends. He wants you to be part of His family, and desires to be your best friend. He is the best friend anyone can have. He is forever faithful, and always listening to his children.

PRAYER

Dear Lord, I know I am a sinner. I ask you to remove and cleanse me of my sins. Wash me clean with your blood. Please come into my life. I give you my heart and soul. I believe you died for me and that we will be together for eternity. I surrender my way for your way. Teach me your ways. Keep me from temptation and evil.

By faith I cancel all demonic authority in my life. Devil, you have to go now, you are no longer welcome here.

Jesus, I thank you for being here for me. I confess that now you are my Lord. In the name of Jesus I pray. Amen.

About the Author

J. Katherine Till

J. Katherine Till is a writer enthusiast who writes non-fiction books. Her present repertoire consists of two ghost books, which contain true accounts of hauntings she and her family members have encountered over the years.

The author is a born-again believer in Christ, and she enjoys sharing her Christian faith with others. She is a prayer warrior and has been involved in many spiritual battles. Through the grace of God, and as a result of prayer, people have been set free from spiritual and physical bondages. She has seen many miracles and witnessed lives transformed by the power of God.

Till's passion for writing began as a teenager, and her life experiences have helped to develop that creativity. Some college education, and much writing over the years, have helped to prepare her for this endeavor.

To contact the author write to:

J. Katherine Till
P.O. Box 1
Norfork, AR 72658

Or send an e-mail to:

bookendspublications@yahoo.com

Ghost Books
by J. Katherine Till

Swamped by Ghosts contains true accounts of spirit encounters my family members and I have had from our childhood to the present.

Haunted House of the Rising Sun is about a beautiful mansion in the New Orleans area that I lived in with my first husband and our two children. What started out as a dream come true became more like a nightmare as we witnessed hauntings almost every day of the four years we lived there. Many mysterious things happened that could not be explained.

My Parade of Ghosts will be published soon. It begins when I remarry and move in with my new husband and his two children. I hope to never encounter the paranormal again, but soon realize that the house is infested with ghosts. It takes me on a journey that I do not wish to go on.

Like a parade procession, this series describes a series of hauntings which occurred one after another over several years and in the various homes I have lived in. The books draw the reader through several cities and four states, which include the Mardi Gras city of New Orleans. But this parade isn't one of fun and celebration. It is a series of frightening spirit encounters.

These books all have a last page. They end. I would like to have a closure to the paranormal phenomena I am experiencing, but I continue having ongoing encounters with spirits.

After writing my first ghost book, I researched ghostly phenomena and was surprised at the vast amount of just the documented accounts throughout America. I was relieved to know that other people have had similar experiences to mine. This knowledge helps me to better understand and deal with the spirit encounters I have had.

I hope you have enjoyed reading *Swamped by Ghosts* and that it helps you in some way.

To order copies of this book, go to Amazon.com and search for *Swamped by Ghosts* by J. Katherine Till.

Joseph and Angela Adair

The nature photos in this book are the work of Joseph Adair. To purchase copies of Joseph Adair's array of nature photos, you may contact him at joanatrio@yahoo.com.

Joseph Adair and his wife Angela are authors of the non-fiction book *Louisiana: Eroding Treasures*, which can be purchased at www.lulu.com and www.amazon.com.

Joseph Adair

Joseph and his wife, Angela.